BETH THROUGH TIME

BETH THROUGH TIME

A *Magical Bookshop* Novel

HARMKE BUURSMA

ISBN 978-1-7374033-7-1 (hardcover dustjacket)
ISBN 978-1-7374033-8-8 (ebook)
ISBN 978-1-17374033-9-5 (paperback)

Edited by Megan Sanders
Author photo by Patterson Photography
Cover design by Getcovers.com

Published by Illusive Press
info@illusivepress.com
www.illusivepress.com

For more information about Harmke Buursma and her books, visit
www.harmkebuursma.com

First Edition, 2022

For love, in all its many different forms

Contents

Quote

"To be fond of dancing was a certain step towards falling in love."
- Jane Austen, Pride and Prejudice

I

The London Season

"I am glad to be in London," I told Anne as we exited the carriage. The driver stopped in front of a tall, tan building; the place near Covent Garden we would call home for the next couple of months. I could not wait to explore the open-air market and everything else London had to offer.

Anne locked her arm with mine and flashed me a smile. "I can scarcely believe your brother is sponsoring my season." She lifted her brows and smiled ruefully at me. "To think I'll be attending the balls, parties, and al fresco picnics along with you after I thought I'd have to stay behind in Westbridge this year."

My brother, John, and his wife, Rose, swerved past us to greet the butler who had opened the front door of the charming townhouse. The beige stonework was livened up with white painted window frames and trellises with creeping ivy.

"Welcome, sir," the middle-aged man said, bowing his head, revealing neatly combed, silver hair.

"What is your name?" John asked.

"Bartley, sir." The butler had a deep soothing voice.

"Good afternoon, Bartley. Could you send out a footman to bring in our belongings?" John pointed to the luggage at his feet and the other suitcases and bags the carriage driver was currently placing near the open cast-iron gate in front of the tan facade.

"Right away, sir," the butler said. He motioned at a young gangly man behind him who hurried out to retrieve the luggage. The footman barreled past us with his head ducked and lifted the first of the suitcases. He barely lifted his freckled face to look at us.

I glanced up at the townhome, letting out a breath, aware of the smile that was growing on my face. The anticipation of everything that could happen in London energized me after the long carriage ride. I grinned at Anne. "I am glad you will be my companion and," I winked, "my partner in crime."

Anne rolled her eyes and let out an exaggerated sigh. "I should have known. What are you planning now?"

I feigned innocence, clutching my hand to my chest in mock affront. "Me? Nothing at all."

Anne burst into a throaty laugh. "You forget that I know you. You always have some kind of plan."

"Do not let John hear you." I leaned into Anne so I could whisper in her ear. "I mean to make the most of my first Season and could use your help with running interference."

Anne bumped her hip against mine, snorting. "As long as you don't get me into trouble, promise?"

I wiggled my brow. "I promise."

Anne shuffled her legs and bit her lip. "I just don't want to disappoint your brother. He is entirely too generous to let me stay with you and purchase my wardrobe for the season. My family cannot possibly repay him, not even with my brother teaching at Rose's school."

She raised her shoulders and hesitated. "And my behavior has not been... well. You are aware."

I was. She had been dishonest in the past when she tried to snare my brother into matrimony, hurting Rose, my brother's now wife, in the process.

"What I did then..." Anne frowned and stared at her fingertips. "I truly regret behaving in that kind of manner."

"Rose and John have forgiven you. We are all aware of your circumstances and do not blame you for it."

Anne sniffed. "Regardless."

"Do not worry about that. We will not be upsetting my brother; I'm not planning a coup. I merely want the chance to meet and dance with a few fetching gentlemen. Knowing my brother, he's planning to keep a close watch on me and deter any and all suitors. I love him, but he can be overbearing." I smiled, glancing back at my brother and his wife. "Rose has helped lighten him up, but still..."

Anne snorted. "You're his baby sister. He still imagines you as the young girl in pigtails, the girl he had to raise after..." She stopped her sentence.

I shrugged. "I understand why he acts the way he does; although, it doesn't take away the fact that I am nearly twenty-one years old. A few more years and I shall practically be a spinster." I shuddered at the thought. My foiled elopement last year with the dreadful Mr. Danby had been a mistake, but I had grown more mature, and I wanted to be out in the world. I envied my brother and Rose's relationship. And William and Austin's.

I did not necessarily want to get married yet, but I did want to experience life and love for myself. Attending the London season gave me the best opportunity to do so. I would get to mingle and dance with eligible bachelors, meet new friends, and the shopping would not hurt either.

Estelle, carrying her own suitcase, caught up with us. The French ladies' maid was the only staff member from Hawthorne to come with us, partly because I relied on her skills with my hair. I wanted to be certain Anne and I would be dressed and coiffed per my standards. But also, because I considered her a friend and wished her to enjoy some experiences outside of our country estate.

Anne and I climbed the few steps to the front door as the butler invited John and Rose inside.

The butler pointed his hand away from the main staircase. "I will show you the way to the drawing room while the staff readies the bed-chambers for you and your party."

The five of us followed Bartley from the foyer into the hallway, a plush red carpet rolled out beneath our feet. To our right, we entered the drawing room, a bright and airy space. Anne's face lit up as she spotted the piano forte in the corner of the room. Translucent white drapes reached down from the ceiling, framing wide windows which bathed the room in sunlight and brought attention to a weaved carpet covering the wood floor. From Brussels, I deduced, noting the intricate multi-colored pattern.

Estelle excused herself and followed the butler to the servants' area. Rose swished past me and planted herself on the love seat, sighing as she sank into the velvet upholstery.

"This is a nice place," she said, staring up at her husband. John's eyes trained on his wife, a smile playing at his lips. Rose patted her hand on the spot next to her.

"Only the best for my sweet," my brother said as he crossed the room and joined Rose. John turned to me as I found a seat of my own. "Before we left for London, I received an invitation from Mr. Brocklehurst and his wife. They are asking us to attend a luncheon with them at Hyde Park later this week.

"Hyde Park?" Anne said, perking up beside me. "Will we take a turn on Ladies' Mile?"

Rose quirked her head inquisitively. "Ladies' Mile?"

Anne nodded. "It's a gentle route through Hyde Park where women ride their horses or men show off their fancy carriages. I spent quite a few afternoons there last year, people-watching and being taken on pleasure rides."

"Perhaps John can take us around the Ladies' Mile before we head towards our meeting place with Mrs. Brocklehurst then," Rose said.

I was glad Rose and Anne were getting along better. Their interactions had been stilted since Rose arrived out of nowhere and caught John's attention. I didn't blame Anne for wanting to marry my brother; I recognized that he'd been a catch, but I was glad he had chosen Rose. Anne never loved my brother, and now that there no longer was any competition or rivalry between Rose and Anne, our friendship had gotten closer. I hoped Rose and Anne would eventually become friends as well. I had high hopes, especially since the idea of sponsoring Anne's season came from Rose, all so John would feel secure in the knowledge that I had a chaperon present at all times.

I touched the leaves on a fern decorating a side table. My mind buzzed with excitement. London. I was truly here. My coming out into society was finally happening. I could not wait to attend all the fetes in my new wardrobe. I peeked up from the fern and returned my hand to my lap before I accidentally tore off pieces from the plant.

"When shall Anne and I visit the modiste?"

John crossed his leg and considered for a moment. "I suppose we can venture out tomorrow if both of you are up to it." He turned to Rose. "Would you like to go shopping with me while Anne and Beth attend their dress fittings?"

Rose rolled her neck, stretching her muscles. "I reckon a good night's sleep will get me back to being as fit as a fiddle. I have to say this trip felt more uncomfortable than usual. My behind is stiff from sitting on the same bench for hours."

John smirked. "Aging prematurely?"

Rose swatted his shoulder. "Do I need to remind everyone about your loud snoring."

I hid a grin. My brother and Rose loved teasing each other, but I could tell it was good-natured. One only needed to pay attention to the way John gazed at his wife to understand that he loved her deeply. I wondered if I would ever have someone to gaze at me the same way, as if I was the most important thing in the world.

John grabbed a newspaper from the side table and, licking the tip of his finger, opened it up to the first page. I caught a glimpse of the front page; a crude drawing of a man next to the title "Gentleman Thief Strikes Again."

"Why does that sound familiar?" I mused out loud.

"Hmm?" John glanced up from the paper.

I pointed at the cover. "That headline sounded familiar."

John scanned the text. "Ah, yes. No wonder. It was during William's trial; a man nicknamed the Gentleman Thief was amongst the other prisoners waiting to be heard by the judge."

Yes, that was it. I hadn't seen his face, but now I remembered the posters plastered all over the courthouse.

We were interrupted by the butler returning with tea. John flipped to the next page while Bartley doled out cups and started pouring the fragrant liquid.

"None for me, please. I would like to retire soon."

The butler straightened into his formal stance. "The rooms have been readied, miss."

I jumped up out of the chair, thanking the butler. "If you will excuse me. I shall go explore the rest of the house and pick my room."

John shook his head and laughed. "As long as you do not pick the largest one."

I quirked my brow. "First come, first served." I glanced to Anne. "Would you like to investigate our rooms together?"

Anne nodded and stood. Together, we left the drawing room while John caressed Rose's shoulder and handed her a cup of tea.

"This is a comfortable place," I told Anne, as we trudged up the hardwood stairs. "It is not as familiar or comfortable as Hawthorne, but whoever decorated the place spared no expense on the decor." My feet sank into the thick carpeting covering every tread.

We skipped the first floor which held two adjoining rooms that could be turned into a larger suite—which John and Rose had claimed before arriving—and continued on to the second floor. There, Anne and I chose our rooms; I picked the bedchamber with a view overlooking the street. I leaned against the sill, spying out the window. Below, curricles and coaches passed by while random men and women scurried along the sidewalk as they headed to whatever their destination was. I could not wait to be amongst these strangers, strolling along the streets, exploring the shops, taking in every sight.

The floor creaked behind me, and I swirled around to see my friend enter my room.

"Oh, Anne. Are you not excited to be in London?"

An amused smile played at her lips. "I think you forgot that I experienced my fair share of London seasons."

I brushed past her, planting myself on the bed, and leaned back on my palms. "Tell me, then, are the gatherings much grander than the parties in Westbridge?" I observed Anne as she considered my question, tapping a slender finger against her chin.

"Well, there are many more people attending, everyone dressed in the latest fashions. It is wonderful to mingle and dance with gentlemen from more faraway parts."

I nodded, understanding. "It does get dull to dance with the same three or four men at a ball in Westbridge. There's no excitement when you grew up with them and remember when they were going through their awkward stages." I smirked. "Do you remember Milton's boils?"

Anne snorted. "He still requests a dance at every gathering. I truly hope Mother never considers him to be an equal match."

"The only fun and exciting party in Westbridge had been Mrs. Ashbrook's masquerade, and John just let me attend that for the first time last year." I stood from the bed, spreading my skirts and bowing to Anne.

"I want a dashing gentleman to sweep me off my feet, someone tall and muscular with a strong jawline."

I grasped Anne's hand as she giggled. "Are those your only requirements?"

I winked. "I shall think of more. Of course, he would introduce himself and kiss my perfectly gloved hand." I pulled Anne's hand towards me and brushed my lips across them. "Then he'd lead me to the dance floor, and we would waltz the entire evening."

Anne shook her head but went along with my play acting. I pulled Anne closer at the waist, and we danced circles across the floor of my bedchamber. Anne burst out laughing at the final round.

"And what next?" Anne hiccoughed, brushing away a tear from the crook of her eye.

I smirked. "Well, I suppose I would let him kiss me."

At this, she laughed louder. "Do not let your brother catch wind of your plans. I have a feeling John would lock you in your room and throw away the key."

I exhaled deeply. "Probably." Anne shot me an amused

smile. I shrugged. "Oh, alright, most likely. But it is a fine fantasy regardless."

"Romance is a wonderful notion," Anne mused, staring off to the side. She had stopped laughing and her shoulders seemed to deflated a bit. "I wonder if I will get the chance to..." she sighed. "I suppose I should not think about what could be. Mother told me to do my best to find a husband this year." Anne let go of me and moved to the bed. "You know our finances are strained, and if I do not marry well... cannot be certain we could stay where we are."

My voice softened as I sat next to her. "Not even with your brother earning wages while teaching at Rose's school?"

She shrugged again; her expression clouded over. "Perhaps But what about when Rose takes over once more?"

"I am certain John could..." I started.

Anne grimaced. "I dislike taking his charity... your charity There are not enough words to explain how grateful I am but I am indebted to you. I am not deserving of this kindness after the way I treated John and Rose."

"None of us hold it against you."

"Which somehow makes me feel worse." Anne let out a dry chuckle. "I am sorry, I do not mean to sound ungrateful."

I brushed her comment aside and hugged her. "You do not need to worry about sounding ungrateful. You can share what is on your mind with me. Do you not consider me your friend?"

"Of course, I do. I am grateful for your friendship," Anne muttered against my ear.

I moved back, staring up at her with a grin. "Besides it means we are both hunting for handsome bachelors this season. Who is to say we could not both return to Westbridge with a romantic partner?"

2

An Encounter At The Modiste

The next morning, all of us, including Estelle, headed out to the shops. A tawny-haired man in his mid-twenties—the coachman in service to the house John was letting—drove us to Leicester Square. I insisted on exploring a different shopping area than the fashionable Bond Street, and this location was conveniently close.

The driver was attentive as he held open the carriage doors for us to disembark. He held a certain charm which didn't go unnoticed by Estelle, judging by the scarlet creeping up her cheeks. She grasped his hand to step out on the street. He tipped his hat and flashed the French maid a grin before inclining his head towards John and Rose.

John nodded back before turning to me. "How long do you think you and Anne will need at the modiste?"

My gaze flitted to Anne, thinking. "Perhaps two hours."

"Alright. Rose and I will walk around the square, take in the sights, and in two hours, we will check in at the modiste. To give ourselves a bit of leeway, let us agree to three hours before we return to the townhouse?" Anne and I bobbed our heads. John turned and addressed the driver. "Can you meet us back at this spot in three hours?"

The tawny-haired man bobbed his head. "Yes, sir. I will be waiting here." Then, he climbed back into the driver's seat.

John slid his hand into his pocket, pulling out a wallet. "This should do to cover the expenses." He opened the wallet and handed me a few of the bank notes inside. I grasped the currency and added them to my velvet reticule. John winked to me and clasped Rose's hand. "Have fun." Then my brother and Rose took off.

"Let us find the modiste," I told Anne and Estelle. The French maid's eyes were bright and excited. I guessed that Estelle enjoyed the chance to visit London and join Anne and myself on our trip to the modiste.

Tall storefronts and bright signs flanked one side of the sidewalk while on our other side was a bustling street, carriages and single riders passing us by as we walked along the pavement. I liked staring at the different signs and storefronts; it reminded me of a time when my mother was still alive.

My mother loved shopping and often brought me along to stores, calling me her little shadow because I would always cling to her side. I had to touch everything she tried on, smooth silks slipping through my tiny fingers. No one was as beautiful or as graceful as my mother when she swished her skirts and turned about, just so, while admiring her new outfit.

I inherited my love of fashion from her.

Anne, Estelle, and I passed several stores before turning a corner. There, at the end of the street, was the entrance to our location. The gentle tinkling of a bell announced our arrival into the modiste's shop.

A striking woman with large brown eyes and glossy auburn hair pulled up in curls assessed us. "Welcome," she said, stepping from behind the register. "Are you here for a fitting?"

The outside of the dress shop had been painted a reserved brown, but inside, the space burst with colors. Stands with a variety of hats stood next to the register and rolls of fabric hung from a display on the wall. Everywhere you looked there was another accessory to discover; plumes of feathers which would go perfect in a hairdo, fake fruits to be added to hats, and delicate pieces of lace ready to be sewn to the hems of muslin gowns. The interiors of dress shops were a world of wonder.

I smiled and pointed to Anne and myself. "Indeed. My companion and I are intending to purchase a new wardrobe for the season."

"You are in luck. There is only one other customer currently being fitted, so we can accommodate the space for your party. We usually are rather busy this time of year." The auburn-haired woman's eyes flitted to Estelle, her nose lifting. "Does your other companion need any help?"

I thought of what needed to be purchased. With John's notes now filling my purse there should be plenty to go around, and Estelle did not leave Hawthorne very often.

"Yes, my ladies' maid would also like a new dress made."

"Non, Miss Easton," Estelle spluttered. "I don't need a new dress. It is too much." She seemed shocked that I would include her in our plans.

I laid my hand on her shoulder. "You deserve a new dress. Besides, you will want to wear something fetching when you accompany Anne and myself somewhere. Though, if you insist, it can be something practical."

Estelle bit back another response, hesitation warring on her face. But, seeing my delighted expression, the crease on her forehead softened and she nodded. "Thank you, made-moiselle."

I turned to the shop lady. "Perhaps a pretty day dress for my ladies' maid."

The modiste inclined her head. "Certainly." She motioned to another shop girl. The new girl, a sprightly young woman, welcomed Estelle and led her to the wall of fabrics in the front while the auburn-haired woman led Anne and myself through an archway in the back of the store into a fitting area hidden by velvet drapes.

Another woman was already there being draped in different yards of fabric by her short, older chaperon, pins sticking out at key placements. I estimated her to be around my age with a beautiful soft figure and thick, red hair. The modiste, who had led us inside, passed her by, then stopped and turned to me.

"This will do. You can call me Ms. Taylor while I help you and your companion." Anne and I nodded. Ms. Taylor smiled. "Now, do you ladies have any preferences in color, cut, or style?" She counted on her fingers.

"Whatever is the current fashion," I suggested.

From the other corner of the room the lady being fitted grumbled to the chaperon assisting her.

I thought back to the adverts I had seen about fashion from Europe, rubbing my chin. "Perhaps scalloped hemlines or dual-toned muslin? Or even a sweetheart neckline instead of the square neckline?"

The red-haired woman stumbled as she pulled away a swath of fabric, catching herself by pressing her palm against the papered wall. A high-pitched yelp escaped her and another shop girl scurried towards her, adjusting the pins around the woman's bust.

"I apologize, miss. Let me change those for you." The woman swatted the shop girl's hand away, scowling. "I do not like being poked and prodded like a pig for slaughter. Could you please take those pins and that fabric away?"

Anne and I glanced at each other. Amusement glimmered in Anne's eyes. A small smirk formed on my face before I forced my expression to obey so I could pay attention to the modiste. Anne coughed softly, hiding a laugh behind her hand.

Ms. Taylor remained calm as she focused on us. "Those are interesting ideas; I can certainly consider them." The modiste smiled pleasantly. "If you ladies can spare a moment, I shall fetch a selection of different fabrics." She turned and left through the archway.

"Are we almost finished?" the red-headed lady asked her chaperon. She frowned as the shop girl held different colors of fabric up to the side of her face. "I do not want or need a new dress."

From a small ottoman, her chaperon tutted. "Ms. Willa, your father has given me clear instructions to see to it you are fitted with a new wardrobe and accompanying accessories. It is important you make a good impression."

The shop girl assisting the lady hesitated, clearly uncomfortable with the situation. I did not understand why the woman named Willa did not want a new dress. The process of getting fitted, seeing the transformation with every new fabric, was something I enjoyed. The shop girl held up a beautiful forest green silk fabric next to the woman's hair. The color went well with her red coloring, but the woman remained unyielding, staring straight ahead with a frown of displeasure.

Her chaperon tutted and snatched the fabric from the shop girl's hands. "Ms. Willa, can you truly not be pleased to receive a new dress? Think of your father and how proud he would be to see you in it."

"Proud enough to get rid of me," Willa retorted with a snort. The chaperon laid the fabric across Willa's shoulder, followed by the shop girl who pulled out various lace pieces and trims to match from a drawer behind her.

"That color suits you," I told the red-headed woman. She turned her head, her gaze calculating, though she flashed me a genuine smile.

"Thank you," she said, before squinting at the shop girl. "You can take that one away. I need something unflattering, orange perhaps."

Anne's mouth popped open, and I stifled a giggle.

The red-haired lady shot me a grin while her chaperon

rolled her eyes and sighed. "What am I supposed to say to your father?"

Smirking, she told her chaperon, "Tell him I have received a new wardrobe just as he wanted." She turned to us. "Father is pressuring me to join the marriage mart this year, but I have no intention of marrying anyone."

"Is this your first year? My brother did not want me to go, but I finally got him to agree." I pointed to my friend. "Anne has attended the London season a few times."

"It is my first year," the red-haired lady nodded. "But father is dead-set on getting me engaged and out of his hair."

The chaperon gasped. "Willa."

"Yes, I know." Willa rolled her eyes. "He's doing it for my own good, and all that nonsense."

"We are in the company of others," the chaperon reminded, pursing her lips.

"We are all ladies here," the red-haired woman said. She stepped towards us and extended her hand. "My name is Willa."

"Beth," I greeted her.

"Anne."

Willa smiled. "Perhaps we will run into each other at one ball or another."

The shop girl returned, a horrid orange-brown fabric clasped in her hands. Willa's face brightened as she took in the garish color.

"Perfect. That will do nicely. Let us return home," she told her chaperon. "I am tired of being poked and prodded." On her way out, she glanced at us. "It was nice to meet you both."

Once Willa left, we had the fitting room to ourselves. I

enjoyed standing on the raised platform while a shopgirl took my measurements. Ms. Taylor helped Anne and me pick out new day dresses and evening gowns for the balls and parties we were sure to attend. The new clothes would be delivered to our townhouse at Covent Garden later this week, together with Estelle's new day dress.

John and Rose were waiting for us when we exited.

"Did you find what you both needed?" John asked.

"Yes, thank you," Anne said.

"The modiste had a good selection of fabrics," I told John. "Though the most exciting part was the other customer."

"Oh?" John smiled.

"Yes, she was dead set on purchasing an unflattering dress despite her chaperon's protestations."

My brother laughed and quickly glanced at his wife before telling me, "Perhaps I should order the same for you. It might deter some future suitors."

I crossed my arms. "You promised you would not interfere in my first London season."

"Oh Beth, do not look so stern." John laughed and shook his head. "I promise I will try my best not to.

* * *

Three days later, a stack of packages arrived from the modiste. Our butler, Bartley, carried them into the dining room where Rose, John, Anne, and I were breaking our fast.

I tapped my spoon along the top of a boiled egg, breaking the shell, while the butler laid the packages down on top of the buffet cabinet, a wide mahogany piece with golden filigree on its doors.

"Thank you, Bartley," John said in between bites of toast.

I dipped a piece of bread into the still soft yolk, savoring the creamy richness.

"If that will be all, sir," Bartley said, tipping his head.

"Yes, we shall manage for now." John smiled heartily at the butler.

I swallowed the bite of food and patted my lips with a napkin before speaking. "It seems with the arrival of our new dresses, Anne and I are ready to join our first outings. Have we received any invitations, brother?"

John handed Rose a bowl of sugar. "Yes, I believe I mentioned the Brocklehursts' invitation earlier this week. They have asked us to join them at Hyde Park for an al fresco luncheon tomorrow."

Anne straightened beside me, excitement flashing in her eyes. "Will we go promenading?"

"I am certain we shall find the time after our luncheon," John said.

Rose nodded as she stirred a cube of sugar into her tea. "Maybe we can go for a carriage ride, since you all seemed so excited about taking a ride along the Ladies' Mile." She chuckled before blowing on her tea. "I kind of want to experience it now too."

"I wonder if we will be able to spot the royal family, perhaps the Prince of Wales or the Duke of York will be out for a ride," Anne mused.

"I suppose there is always a chance," John said.

I grinned. "Oh, would that not be marvelous? Our first outing of the season and we would get to see the prince. Do you think he is handsome?"

Anne munched on a piece of fruit while thinking. "Well, princes are supposed to be dashing, so I am certain he is. Even if only from afar," she added after a brief pause, earning a snort from John.

The luncheon with the Brocklehursts would be the first outing of my first London season. I was thrilled to go out and display my new wardrobe in public, and the merriment was only just beginning. I had months of dances and parties to look forward to, events where—with the help of Anne—my brother would not be keeping a close watch on me.

"I wonder if Queen Charlotte visits Hyde Park with the King," I said.

"I sincerely doubt it," John said. "As far as I heard, the King hardly leaves the palace, let alone his room."

"Even so, I wonder which members of the ton we might encounter tomorrow."

John shot an exasperated glance at Rose who laughed. "More than likely we will only converse with Mr. Brocklehurst's great big mustache."

3

Hyde Park

We arrived at Hyde Park to find Mr. Brocklehurst with a clean-shaven face instead of the generous mustache the man usually sported.

"His barber said it would make him appear ten years younger," Mrs. Brocklehurst twittered to John and Rose while Mr. Brocklehurst traced his fingers along his upper lip. "Can you tell? I do think it makes a vast difference."

John and Rose feigned interest and nodded politely.

I stood beside Anne, fanning myself with a feathered hand fan while wishing I had brought a parasol as sweat beaded at my temples and rolled down the nape of my neck. The sun beat down on us on what was an unseasonably hot day for England.

The Brocklehursts' valet laid out a blanket near the base of a tree which provided some much-needed shade as well as being a perfect spot from which we were able to observe the

Serpentine River and all the visitors walking along the gravel paths at Kensington Gardens.

Arabella, Fanny, and Letitia stood by their mother's side, lined up from eldest to youngest while their father spoke to John.

"Nice to see you again," Arabella told Anne and me while swishing her pale green dress. The eldest daughter looked most like her mother; a pinched look to her cheeks, a small upturned nose, and thin eyebrows above her dark eyes. The middle daughter, Fanny, was the prettier of the three with a soft face and rosy cheeks and lips. Letitia, the youngest at about sixteen, clasped her hands in front of her, a smile on her lips. Her choice of dress and the small ringlets on her forehead made her seem a lot younger than her actual age.

"It has been a while," I said to Arabella, Fanny, and Letitia. I made sure to flash each of them a smile while fanning myself. With today's heat, I was glad that I had chosen to wear my hair up.

The Brocklehursts' valet busied himself with unpacking food and drinks from a wicker basket.

My brother was speaking with Mr. Brocklehurst about William Chambers, my brother's best friend, and Austin Miller, a time-traveler like Rose—although no one except for our immediate family and friends were aware of that. William and Austin had traveled to the future only two months before, with help from the magical bookshop owner, Melinda, after being accused of sodomy by a swindler by the name of Captain Tremblay.

"And where are Mr. Chambers and Mr. Miller? I cannot recall hearing much after that whole affair with Mr. Chambers and his false arrest." Mr. Brocklehurst tutted. "To believe I invited Captain Tremblay into my home. You could not imagine my shock and dismay when I heard the news about how he swindled people out of their money. And to blame it on your dear friend, along with those... other allegations." He coughed delicately.

"Yes, we were all deceived by the man," John said. "But by Jove, justice prevailed, and Captain Tremblay is now spending many years behind bars paying for his crimes."

Mr. Brocklehurst let out a hearty, "Hear, hear."

"You might remember that Mr. Miller, like myself, is from the Americas," Rose said. "He and Mr. Chambers decided to take leave of Westbridge to travel to Mr. Miller's birthplace, though they planned to make several stops along the way."

I listened to Rose and my brother's excuses for William's absence. William had not been gone long, but I missed having him around, and I supposed I even missed his partner Austin, though I did not know him for long. Rose was telling the Brocklehursts the story we came up with to explain why William had left England. I supposed it was not far from the truth. William and Austin had traveled, only the distance measured years not miles. Two hundred years to be exact.

I sometimes wondered what the future would be like, if William and Austin were happy. If I would ever see them again, and whether a certain strange, brown-haired woman would show up in Westbridge once more.

"Let us take a seat," Mrs. Brocklehurst said, pointing towards the blanket. The valet had finished setting out the food and now retreated to stand watch and wait for any other orders to be issued.

I settled in between Anne and Mrs. Brocklehurst's eldest daughter, Arabella, on the checkered blanket. Mrs. Brocklehurst ordered her daughters to hand out cool glasses of lemonade, I was grateful to accept one from Arabella.

"Is this your first time joining the season?" I asked her.

Arabella took a sip from her glass. "This will be my second time, but Mama is set on making a match for me this year. Did you go last year?"

"Yes. This is my third time," Anne said at the same time as I muttered no. "Mr. Easton was so kind as to sponsor my season this year," Anne said.

"Third?" Arabella went owl-eyed. "And still no match?"

Anne blushed and stared down at the ground. "The right suitor has not come around, yet."

"That is right, my dear," Mrs. Brocklehurst said magnanimously. She had been listening in to our conversation. "One should never settle for a subpar suitor. Just take me for instance, happily married with three beautiful daughters. If I settled for the first village boy who asked for my hand in marriage, I might now be married to a husband without the funds to maintain his family. No, I did well to wait for a suitable match."

"Yes, darling," Mr. Brocklehurst said.

"Now you said this is your first year out on the marriage mart?" Mrs. Brocklehurst honed in on me.

"Ms. Blakeley will be her chaperon as well as attend the season herself," John said.

Mrs. Brocklehurst nodded as she scrutinized my appearance. "How old are you, girl?"

"Almost twenty-one."

Mrs. Brocklehurst gasped, appalled. "Nearly twenty-one and this is her first time on the marriage mart?" She shot John a dour glance. "Oh my, Ms. Easton should have been introduced to society years ago. But I suppose with only a brother to take charge of her...her late start can be excused. After all, most men are not aware of the finer points we ladies must contend with." She smiled graciously at us.

"I suppose not," John added, gritting his teeth.

Rose cut in. "So, Mrs. Brocklehurst, are there any suitors for Arabella?" I applauded Rose for her quick thinking because based on John's darkening gaze, my brother was fuming. Mrs. Brocklehurst's words must have hit a nerve despite his best efforts to hide his exasperation.

"Well, I should not say since nothing is final," Mrs. Brocklehurst mused, looking proud. "But... why not. We are amongst friends." She lowered her voice as if it would make us strain harder to glean her gossip. "A Lord Reeves has been asking about my Arabella. Apparently, he's a keen hunter with a sizable swath of land up north. He heard about our hunting grounds and the loveliness of our daughter from a mutual acquaintance."

"How wonderful," I said with as much sincerity as I could muster.

Mrs. Brocklehurst appeared pleased about the idea of Arabella marrying a lord. "As for my other daughters, I decided for Fanny and Letitia to also join the marriage mart this year."

Letitia, the youngest daughter, preened the small curls framing her forehead.From what I remembered she was around sixteen but judging by her appearance she might as well be thirteen or fourteen. She was a short, thin girl with a soft round face and expressive eyes. I could not imagine her dancing with any of the eligible men at a ball.

I set aside my empty glass. The valet swooped in to take away the glassware and disbursed plates with a variety of small bites and sandwiches to everyone in attendance.

Mr. Brocklehurst patted his chin with a kerchief. "Say, John, while the women attend their soirees and parties, why not join me one of these days for a game of cards. You should be acquainted with most of the men I play with; they frequent my estate often to hunt for grouse."

"I will consider it," John said.

I nibbled on a pastry while glancing over at the gravel pathways. Men and women of all social classes strolled past; young boys hocking the latest papers, ladies and their ladies' maids carrying dainty parasols, dandies striding along in their colorful outfits. John tended to disavow the overdecorated menswear, calling it frivolous, though William had a penchant for wearing elaborate vests and kerchiefs.

"—Beth." Anne nudged me.

"Hmm?"

"Mrs. Brocklehurst asked you a question."

"Oh, I do apologize," I told the woman.

Mrs. Brocklehurst lifted her chin and nodded in an all-knowing manner. "It is the heat, I say, I can't recall it ever being this hot so early in the season." Mrs. Brocklehurst snapped her fingers to alert her valet. "Thompson, can you refill our glasses." She pointed a long finger at the glassware which sat empty near the pitcher of lemonade.

"Right away, Mrs. Brocklehurst."

"Now, where was I...? Yes, Beth, which ball are you attending for your first public outing?"

"I-I haven't thought about it. I would need to consider the invitations we received."

Mrs. Brocklehurst turned to Rose. "It is important to consider these things. The right event can make a difference in a woman's future prospects."

"Mama received invitations for Lady Westham's ball," Letitia said.

Rose smiled at the girl. "It sounds like you are very excited. I hope you and your sisters will have a splendid time." She turned to John. "I believe we received invitations for the same ball, right?"

John nodded. "We did. The butler delivered them yesterday."

"Perhaps Anne and I will see you there," I told Mrs. Brocklehurst's daughters.

The valet handed us our refilled glasses.

"And, Mr. Easton, what about Ms. Blakeley whom you are sponsoring? Did you consider options for her?"

"Now, dear, I'm sure Mr. Easton is doing right by the girl." Mr. Brocklehurst smiled at his wife.

That my brother managed to keep his thoughts from forming on his face impressed me. He had never made it a secret that he disliked Mr. And Mrs. Brocklehurst; "a couple of braggarts," he called them in private. I did not fault their daughters for this; they appeared rather shy and reserved, not that I knew them well. But Mr. and Mrs. Brocklehurst had invited us, and it was in poor form to decline.

Anne scraped her throat. "Mr. And Mrs. Easton are hosting me and secured me a new wardrobe for the season; they are doing everything they can to assure a successful season."

Mrs. Brocklehurst ignored Anne. Instead, her eyes remained targeted on John. "A few of Arabella and Fanny's old suitors, ones we have considered to be below our daughters' standards, might be decent prospects for Ms. Blakeley. Oh, but we have all heard the gossip around town. You know, about the late Mr. Blakeley and his eldest son and what they were up to."

Anne stiffened beside me. I gripped her hand and squeezed it. "Perhaps—"

"Doesn't the younger Mr. Blakeley now work at that quaint school of yours?" Mr. Brocklehurst asked Rose.

"He is excellent with the children of our tenants," Rose said.

Mrs. Brocklehurst's head swiveled to Anne. "Do you still have a dowry?"

Mrs. Brocklehurst was met with silence.

"No? Pity. I could reach out to those old suitors; however, without a dowry…"

"None of that is necessary, Mrs. Blakeley," John said. "I thank you for your kind offer, but I shall assure that Ms. Blakeley will find a proper match, and I will see to it her dowry will be covered."

"Mr. Easton," Anne choked out.

John shook his head at Anne. "I will hear nothing more about the matter." Then he turned his attention to Mr. And Mrs. Brocklehurst. His voice grew cold. "Ms. Blakeley is a part of our household at the moment, and she shall be treated with the same courtesy and respect as my sister."

Mrs. Brocklehurst turned white as a sheet despite whipping her chin up towards the sky to show her indignation. "Indeed." The tension was palpable even to the most oblivious person. "I am merely offering my valuable insights."

Mr. Brocklehurst squirmed from his spot on the blanket, unsure of how to proceed. "What my wife means to say—"

"I think your wife has said enough," John cut in.

Rose drained her glass of lemonade. "This is a refreshing drink; your cook must share their recipe with ours. Am I correct in detecting something besides lemons?" She laid her hand on John's arm, offering him a soft shake of her head. John relaxed.

Mrs. Brocklehurst, eager to end the awkward silence, accepted the change in topic. "Did you know our chef once trained in Italy? According to him, the Italians like to add herbs to their beverages, which is how he picked up the habit and introduced it to us. He tells me he adds sprigs of rosemary when he prepares the lemonade then strains the liquid before serving."

Rose smiled. "Delicious, I will need to share his secret with our cook."

"Mama, Papa, can we go promenading?" Arabella said.

Still a bit flustered, Mrs. Brocklehurst gazed at her daughter. "Once you finish your beverage, and don't stray too far."

The eldest daughter downed her drink as fast as possible while still appearing prim and proper then stood along with her sisters. Anne and I followed, linking our arms together as we traversed the soft grass. I believed we were both glad for a respite from Mrs. Brocklehurst.

We ambled along the path, viewing the different carts

with sweet treats and ladies' accessories while also observing the other men and women strolling through the park. The ones walking past in a hurry tended to be dressed simply in dark colors and unembellished hats, spots of wear and tear visible on the fabric. They were working-class men and women headed to their location of employment. Others strolled around lazily in their finest outfits, enjoying the sunshine as we were, and taking their time glancing over the wares on offer. A small child was licking an ice as he toddled along with his parents.

I glanced at the newspaper boy holding up today's papers.

"Where is the Gentleman Thief? Buy your paper here and find out," the boy shouted. "Only seven pence."

Shrugging, I walked past. I did not need to know, and if there was something interesting, I was certain my brother would tell me over dinner.

The three younger Brocklehursts gathered around a cart with embroidered handkerchiefs. Arabella caressed a cotton square and sighed.

"I wonder what gentleman I will marry. Do you think I will find a match this year?" Her large round eyes turned to us. "I do hope I will marry the lord my papa mentioned. Perhaps we will all find matches and return to Westbridge as married ladies." Her voice trilled in excitement.

"Perhaps," Anne said, her voice flat though she kept her expression even.

Arabella clapped her hands. "Come, let us continue our promenade; there might be men now just waiting to catch a glimpse of us."

I snorted softly, smiling at Arabella. "Of course, you and your sisters can go ahead."

4

Daughter Of A Marquis

My first ball of the London season had finally arrived. Anne and I reached Lord and Lady Westham's manor dressed to impress in our new gowns. I had dreamed of attending since I was a little girl. Now that it was here, I could not help but feel out of my depth. My stomach roiled and sweat slicked my palms. I brushed my hands against the sides of my dress, hoping to wick away the moisture.

My father had met my mother at a ball during the London season. He had fallen in love with her the instant he had laid eyes on her. At least, that is what he used to tell us. I was not certain if I believed in love at first sight, but the notion had always stayed with me. John and Rose had not fallen in love the first time they met, but they were certainly well-matched. I wondered if true love would ever be in the cards for me. The first time I let myself be vulnerable, I was deceived by Mr. Danby.

I swallowed and shook off some of my nerves. Mr. Danby had been arrested, and I would never have to see him again. There was no need for me to worry. I was looking forward to my first ball of the season and my first real taste of freedom.

Anne straightened, lifting her chin and glancing around eagerly as we entered the manor. A footman showed us in and led us across the impressive marble-floored foyer with double staircases into a grand ballroom. Candles illuminated the entire dance floor, warm lights flickering across polished surfaces and elegant wainscoting. I was used to bright colors and textured wallpapers, but Lady Westham's ballroom appeared dream-like precisely because of the lack of vivid color. Every wall was beautifully finished in eggshell, a blank canvas for the craftsmanship to shine.

Groups of dancers already gathered in a large circle at the center of the dance floor, couples moving in tandem, bright skirts swishing in time to the music.

I let out a sigh and pulled out my dance card, still empty for now. But hopefully soon every slot would be filled.

Anne whispered in my ear. "Let us grab a refreshment and wait for introductions to be made." I nodded, worrying my lip. Then, realizing what I was doing, I stopped and smoothed my features into the approachable mask of a gentle woman. I had had some practice in Westbridge. London should be no different. Except it was.

Anne handed me a glass of lemonade. I sipped it slowly, gazing around as casually as I was able to. "Who do you think will approach us first?" I asked Anne, my gaze resting on a sandy-haired man wearing a brocade blue waist coat, before skipping to a broad-shouldered man in highly polished top boots. I wondered if either of them was a good dancer.

"They are probably waiting until they get a chance to be introduced." She nodded in the direction of the musicians. I followed her gaze straight to the figure of lady Westham. The matronly woman was doing rounds, greeting various guests. When she reached the refreshment table, decked out with libations and impressive towers of fruits, her attentions turned to us.

Her eyes flitted across my figure. "Welcome to my home," she said, smiling. "You must be Ms. Easton."

I curtsied, lowering my gaze before answering. "Indeed. I am grateful for the invitation into your wonderful home."

Lady Westhams' gaze turned to Anne. "And who is your companion?"

"This is my friend, Ms. Blakeley. My brother is sponsoring her season this year."

Anne straightened. "It is a pleasure to meet you, Lady Westham."

Lady Westham waved her hand airily. "Nonsense dear, the pleasure is all mine. Enjoy the party," she said, as she continued on her way.

Our introduction was brief, but now that we had been acknowledged by the host, the other guests felt free to approach us.

The broad-shouldered man in top boots requested to be added to both Anne and my dance card, same as the sandy-haired man wearing the blue brocade waist coat.

I was about to finish my lemonade and step out onto the

dance floor when a woman with bright red curls pushed past us and bumped into the refreshments table.

She let out an audible gasp as her hip connected with the heavy top and the tall towers of fruit tumbled down to the ground, mandarins scattering all around her.

I winced in sympathy; that must have hurt.

The woman rubbed her hip, a pinched look on her face, and bent to pick up the fruit.

"Are you alright?" I asked, crouching next to her. She turned to me, frowning at first before recognition flashed across her face.

Now that I saw her up close, I recognized her as well. "Wait, I remember you from the modiste. Willa, right?"

Her eyes crinkled into a smile. "Yes. You were there for my fitting." She picked up mandarins, returning them to the table in haste. "I apologize, I do not have time to speak." She glanced behind her, skin flushing when she noticed the entire room staring at her. "I have got to go." She picked up the last piece of fruit and stood.

"Wait," I called after her, but she ignored me and raced from the room. A few girls were snickering near us, whispering to each other behind their raised hands.

"Let her go," Anne said, grasping my wrist. "We have quadrilles to dance. I'm certain Willa will be fine. That woman is an odd one." Anne's hazel eyes flitted to the hallway where Willa had run off to.

I grimaced, glancing between the spot that Willa had disappeared into and the dance floor where the broad-shouldered man would be waiting for his dance. I wanted to dance, but Willa had seemed distressed. What if she was in trouble and needed help? I might not know her beyond our brief meeting at the modiste, but would I not want someone to look out for me if our roles were reversed? If John and Rose had not come looking for me a year ago, I would have been ruined by Mr. Danby.

"You can go ahead," I told Anne. "I will only be a moment."

"Beth," she said, a warning in her voice. "I am supposed to chaperon you."

"I know, I will not be long. I just want to make certain she is alright. Enjoy a dance for me, please."

She raised her brow and smirked. "Fine, but if you do not hurry, I will dance twice with both men."

"Scandalous, Ms. Blakeley," I whispered in a laugh.

Anne let go of my wrist, and I strode to the hallway as fast as I could without drawing attention to myself. The narrow pathway was quiet except for some soft rustling coming from an open doorway. I found Willa stooped in a study, rubbing at what I assumed was a tender spot on her hip.

"Who is there?" she exclaimed, flipping around to face me. Her expression relaxed when she saw it was me. "Oh. It is you."

"Beth Easton," I said, figuring I needed to reintroduce my-self. I snorted when I noticed the color of her dress.

Willa quirked her brow. "What is so funny?"

"I suppose you were not lying at the modiste when you said you wanted an unflattering wardrobe."

She pulled at the orange-brown colored skirt. "Yes. They had the good sense to listen to me." Willa flashed me a grin before frowning. "Why did you follow me?"

"You seemed flustered. I wanted to make sure you were alright."

She considered me for a moment. "Well, you have seen me. There is nothing wrong with me so you are free to return to the ballroom." She turned and paced around the wide mahogany desk, taking a seat on a leather chair.

I paused. There had to be more to Willa's story, but she did not seem in a hurry to share any information. "Perhaps I can help with whatever it is that is going on," I said.

Willa leaned back, her green cat eyes staring up at me. "I do not think it is anything you can assist me with." I sensed defeat in every syllable. She picked up a quill from the desk, rolling it between her fingers.

"Perhaps," I shrugged. "But we will not know unless we try."

Willa continued fidgeting with the quill. "Can I trust you?" She paused, waiting for my answer, her vivid eyes still focused on me.

"I promise I will not repeat anything you have said here today." Willa's face was so serious. What could possibly be going on for her to be this worried? I did not know what to expect.

Willa sighed, dropping the quill. "Alright. I am hiding from someone."

I frowned. She was hiding? I narrowed my eyes. "Is that someone trying to hurt you? If so, my friend and I can find a way to get you out of here unseen."

Willa smiled and shook her head. "No, it is nothing like that. I have never even met him."

I was confused. "Then what is the problem?"

"The problem is that I did not want to join the marriage mart, but my father forced me to anyways. Then I figured, as long as I keep the suitors away, I would not need to get married. It would not be difficult to keep suitors at bay." Willa laughed wryly. "Little did I know that my father went behind my back and arranged for my engagement to some Irish duke." She shuddered and leaned back against the chair.

I paced the floorboards in front of the desk. Realization flashed through me. "And that is who you are supposed to meet tonight."

"Yes. My first introduction to the Duke of Cashel."

My eyes widened. She had said the title so flippantly despite the fact that it was not every day a duke was in attendance. "A duke?" My voice shot up.

"From Ireland," she answered. "Most likely a middle-aged bore." She sighed. "What am I supposed to do. I do not want to meet him, and he is set to arrive. I overheard the footmen discussing it earlier."

"Are you certain you do not want to meet him? I mean, he is a duke."

"Yes, I am certain," Willa ground out. "Will you help me come up with a plan or not?"

I hesitated. Perhaps Anne had been right and I should return to the ballroom. Did I not want to enjoy myself dancing with eligible men? Instead, I was stowed away in a study together with a woman who wanted to get out of meeting a duke. There was no doubt that most women out here tonight would love to switch places with Willa.

A thought formed in my mind just as Willa flashed her

teeth at me. "What if you take my place?" she shot out, eerily similar to my own idea. But the plan was too simple, it would never work.

"Would he not be able to tell I am not you?"

Willa chewed her fingernail. "He only knows my name. What if we stick together? If someone points me out he would not be able to tell whether it was you or me. Then when he introduces himself, you can take the lead and say your name is Willa Balfour."

"Balfour," I muttered. "But...what if he asks me questions?"

Willa pursed her lips, flicking away a bit of chewed nail. "We are all ladies. I suppose you can entertain him with talk of your own hobbies. If he asks about my father, you can tell the duke that the Marquis of Bambreich is in fine health."

"You are the daughter of a marquis?" I gulped, halting my pacing.

Willa snorted. "For tonight, you are."

"I-I do not know if I should," I said, steadying myself against the desk.

"You cannot turn back now. This will work, I promise," Willa pleaded.

I trained my eyes on her. "But how am I supposed to get rid of him?"

"You can try to dissuade him from courting you or behave badly."

I blanched at that suggestion. "Behave badly? I do not know about that."

Willa shrugged. "Perhaps he will move on if we can deceive him until the end of the London season. I doubt father would have him follow me back to our country estate." She threw up her hands. "I confess, I have not fully thought it through. However, I have faith I can come up with a better solution if I can only avoid meeting him."

There was risk involved, and if I helped Willa, perhaps she could return the favor. "Fine, if I agree to do this, you will have to help as well."

"Anything," she said.

I paused, considering my options. If Willa's father was a marquis, then she might know ways to get invitations to some of the most exclusive events in London.

"Perhaps you can invite my friend and I along to dances attended by the ton?" I would never dream of socializing with a duke or marquis, but perhaps this was a chance to enjoy myself and have conversations with someone handsome and intelligent.

Willa's mouth dropped open. "Why?" She narrowed her eyes. "Do you want to make a better marriage match?"

"This is my first season, and I want to enjoy myself. Though, I suppose my friend is looking for a suitable match," I answered.

"I suppose," she said, lifting her brow. "If that is what you want, though I cannot see the appeal. You have got yourself a deal."

I nodded. "Now what?"

Willa stood and clasped my arm. "We shall return to the ballroom."

"I will have to explain our scheme to my friend so she can help run interference," I warned Willa.

Willa looked me in my eyes. "Can she be trusted to keep a secret?"

"Yes," I answered. Though I knew Anne would certainly chide me in private for joining in on such a harebrained idea.

Willa seemed ready for battle, judging by the determined glint in her eyes. "Are you ready?" she asked. I nodded. "Then let us go."

5

An Irish Duke

Willa and I returned to the ballroom. I signaled Anne who was finishing up a country dance with the broad-shouldered man in top boots. At least my earlier question was answered; the man was in fact not a good dancer. Anne squinted painfully as she dodged his bumbling steps. Her relief was palpable once the song ended and she could move away.

"You may need to find a way to avoid him if your feet are precious to you," Anne warned me as she joined Willa and me.

I flashed a grin. "I saw. You were lucky to come away unscathed." Willa tapped her finger against my shoulder, no doubt to hurry things along. She had a pinched look on her face.

I cleared my throat. "Anne..." I motioned at the red-haired woman. "This is Willa Balfour."

"Yes. We have met." An amused expression crossed Anne's face. "It seems you are feeling better." She fanned herself.

I hesitated; I was unsure of where to start. But Willa stepped forward, her face serious. She inched closer to Anne and lowered her voice. "I am in a bit of a predicament, and Beth has agreed to help me. She will pretend to be me this evening." Anne was on the verge of saying something but Willa continued. "I wish I did not need to ask but would you be willing to help keep up the ruse?" Willa took a hold of Anne's hands. "I would be ever so grateful."

It took everything I had in me to not burst out laughing. I had never seen Anne this lost for words, her mouth flopping open like a fish. Anne shot me a withering glance, which told me I was going to get an earful. I was envious of Willa's bravado, I could use some of her attitude, especially when dealing with my brother.

"Will you?" Willa reiterated, lightly touching Anne's arm.

Anne turned her gaze back to the redhead and inclined her head, scowling slightly. "This does not mean that I agree."

"Thank you," I breathed.

"You are telling me everything when we are back in our rooms," Anne hissed pointedly. "I asked you to not get me in trouble. What would John say?"

I shrugged. "My brother is not here at the moment, and there is no reason for him to find out." The question did hit a nerve. I was not certain this was the best idea either, but I might as well continue on, in for a penny, in for a pound, I supposed. At the very least it would make for an exciting event unless the duke was a terrible bore like Willa assumed.

I was about to suggest we should find ourselves a

refreshment from one of the round tables with beverages and foods scattered throughout the perimeter of the ballroom when the lively chatting quieted and turned into whispers. Every man and woman in the room glanced towards the main entrance. A tall, dark-haired man walked in accompanied by a footman. Lady Westham pushed her way through the crowd to welcome the newcomer, smiling widely.

A mother and her two daughters behind us were whispering intently. "Can you believe it? A duke, here? Perhaps we shall be fortuitous this eve." The mother fussed with the oldest, quickly pinching the girl's pale cheeks to liven them up. "Esther, straighten your posture and smooth out your skirts. Perhaps you can draw his attention—"

The rest of the woman's words were drowned out when I moved my attention to the man now bowing to Lady Westham. So, this was the duke? He was certainly not middle-aged. I took in the cut of his fine clothing; he was trim but strongly built, his muscular thighs displayed in tight fitting beige pantaloons. From the fine finishes on his jacket and elaborately knotted cravat, I surmised that he cared about his appearance. He surely put in a great deal of effort to be the beau of the ball. Not that it mattered, merely the knowledge that he was a duke drew all the attention to him. He could have resembled a slimy toad and society mothers would still have fawned over him. Wealth and titles were most important here.

But now that the man had a title, wealth, and an extraordinarily pleasing countenance...

"Are you certain you want to go through with this?" I asked Willa. Perhaps she'd changed her mind when she noticed that the duke was a handsome young man.

Willa rolled her eyes. "Yes, I am certain. A handsome face is not enough to make me reconsider."

I shook my head and let out a laugh. "I cannot even pretend to understand you." Willa raised her shoulders, uninterested in the man she was supposed to meet.

Fine, if Willa wanted me to pretend to be her then I would. Especially when the evening just got interesting. I stared openly at the duke as he spoke with Lady Westham, his movements measured and refined. He must have asked Lady Westham a question because she glanced to the side, her eyes scanning the room before stopping at the three of us. Then, she pointed her finger towards us. My heart thumped. The duke turned, his dark eyes staring straight at me with the most delicious crooked smile on his face.

I swallowed.

I was being silly; I had met plenty of handsome men. But a part of me whispered, *Did they have those dark piercing eyes? Or that strong jawline?* Flustered, I averted my eyes. Perhaps he was still a bore. That could happen, right?

Willa pinched me. "Ready yourself." Her eyes raked over me, taking in my distracted expression. "Remember... Willa Balfour, the daughter of the Marquis of Bambreich."

I focused on Willa. "The marquis. Yes."

Willa's lips pursed and for a moment she seemed uncertain. Then her eyes darted to the approaching duke and her hesitation vanished.

"Alright. Pretend to have an interesting conversation." Her cat-like eyes locked with Anne. "You, too. Let out a giggle or something. Pretend to be having an amusing conversation."

"I need to act now too? Next, I will receive a position

on Drury Lane." Anne laughed uncomfortably while Willa improvised a story.

"And so, father took us on an outing to the circus. Have you been? Oh la, it was marvelous. Such a unique experience." I was impressed by Willa's ability to make small talk.

I sensed the duke before he arrived. My skin tingled as he neared. His eyes burned a hole against my back, but I ignored the urge to glance over my shoulder and meet his gaze. I threw out a soft giggle at Willa's improvised conversation

"Pardon me." The duke spoke in a warm tone with a seductive Irish lilt. The accent, while attractive, bewildered me. As far as I knew, hardly any of the Irish nobility had any true ties to their country. Perhaps the duke had been raised by an Irish governess. I liked the cadence of it, smooth as syrup with his deep tones.

"May I introduce myself. I am Edmund Humphries, the Duke of Cashel." With his right hand to his heart, he bowed to us.

The three of us curtsied, lowering our gazes. "Well met, Your Grace," I said, once he straightened.

"Our host of the evening told me I could find Ms. Balfour among the three of you." The duke waited for a response. His frame towered over me. I swallowed thickly as I took in his height. I was not short myself so he had to be well over six feet tall. I pulled out my fan, opening the flower design to obscure my face coyly.

"I am Ms. Balfour." I nodded my head at Anne and Willa. "And these are my friends Ms. Blakeley and Ms. Easton." I stuttered slightly at my own name. The lie tangling up my tongue.

"How do you find London?" Willa cut in, giving me time to gather my composure. I pulled my shoulders back and lifted my chin. By the time the duke finished giving his opinion of London, I finalized my act. I was going to play the better version of myself, the funnier, more adventurous, more confident woman I had always wanted to be. If this was going to be a performance I might as well enjoy it.

From my left, I noticed the sandy-haired man wearing the blue brocade striding towards us, on his way to claim the dance on my dance card, no doubt.

I bumped my arm into Anne as casually as I could before turning to the duke.

"Would you care to dance, Your Grace?" I said, flashing a smile. I knew that he should have asked first, but I did not have time to wait. The sandy-haired man knew my name was Easton. Anne and Willa would have to run interference.

The duke quirked his lips. "It would be my pleasure." He extended his arm. I returned the fan to my pocket, grasped his hand, and followed him onto the dance floor. I was acutely aware of the many eyes that followed our interaction. Peeking back to my friends, I saw them waving away the man I had promised a dance. A twinge of guilt bubbled up in my gut. It was not fair to deny him his turn for a dance just to pretend to be someone I was not for Willa.

Willa's reasonings did not even make sense. I would be ecstatic if an Irish duke attended a ball so he could be introduced to me. What was Willa thinking?

The duke led me to the center of the ballroom. Other couples already gathered on the floor, moving to the sweeping melody. He grasped my right hand while the other moved to rest on my waist, pulling me in closer for the waltz.

"Oh," I exclaimed at the small tug. He was standing so close to me, I had to tip my head to look up at his face. The weight of his hand on my hip burned through the fabric, searing itself into my skin.

Glancing up at him, I followed his lead. I always prided myself in being a good dancer, but I'd never danced with a duke before. I was nervous and especially conscious of my clammy hands.

Aware of his gaze, I decided to break the silence. "Do you like to dance, Your Grace?" The duke smiled, revealing straight white teeth. He was probably chuckling at my question. Why did I even ask something so silly? Of course, he did, we were dancing this very moment. The duke could probably sniff out my inexperience with men.

"I do," he stated. "You can tell a lot by the way one dances." His grip on me tightened as he spun me around. What was he insinuating? His brown eyes bored into mine. "You can call me Edmund. Since I have an understanding with you and your father surely, we are on a first name basis?"

"I suppose," I hedged, chewing my lip. My real name almost slipped out before I remembered. "You can call me Willa"

"Well, Willa." The duke repeated the name slowly, savoring it. His grin was wolfish to match his dark hair. A part of me wished it had been my own name on his lips. "Do you like to dance?"

"I do, though I do not get the opportunity often enough."

The duke—Edmund, I corrected in my head—raised his

brow. "And why is that? I would wager that the daughter of a marquis has plenty of opportunities to dance and a long list of suitors to ask her."

I did not want to lie too much. It was easier to keep the story as close to my own as possible. John came to mind. He took on the role of overprotective father when our parents passed away.

"My father is a bit protective of me."

Edmund's brow quirked. "The same father who wrote to a stranger to arrange a marriage match?"

I shrugged, flashing him a stern glower which I usually reserved for my brother. "A marriage contract is different than unvetted suitors at a ball."

Edmund let out a deep laugh. "Point taken." Then he paused. His eyes trained on my face when he asked, "Is an arranged marriage what you want?"

I nearly missed a step. "What?"

The duke repeated his question, slower this time. "Is an arranged marriage what you want?"

"I-I." My voice faltered. I thought of Willa, her pleas to get out of this situation, and I considered how I would feel if I was told I was engaged to a man I had never met.

"No."

Edmund dark eyes assessed me. I lowered my head; I was taken in by this handsome duke, but now the ruse was most likely coming to an end. I felt a strange sensation of loss, my chest squeezing tight. I had a vague ethereal notion of something important moving out of my grasp. My stomach knotted itself up in a ball.

But it was not me the duke was dancing with. If he knew

who I was he never would have given me a second glance. I had nothing to lose and the real Willa wanted nothing to do with him.

Edmund nodded his head. "I can imagine it is difficult to think of oneself married to a complete stranger."

"It is," I agreed

Edmund smiled at me. "Then I propose this; I shall court you as if I was a mere suitor, and if at the end of the season you wish to break off our agreement, I shall step aside."

"Just like that?" I frowned at him. That must be the strangest plan I had ever heard. "Why did you agree to a marriage in the first place?"

"Perhaps I was in want of a wife," he quipped. The music changed, and we were forced to break apart. "However, I would prefer my intended to be excited about her upcoming nuptials."

Heat rose to my cheeks. I turned my head to hide the redness on my face and to catch a glimpse of Anne and Willa. I hated that the idea of marriage to this man was making me blush.

My friends were standing near a refreshment table, Anne sipping from a drink while Willa chomped away at a mandarin. Willa waved and grinned widely when she caught my eye.

"Will you come with me?" the duke whispered in my ear.

I returned my gaze to him. "Where?"

"We can take a stroll in the garden, somewhere we can speak without so many eyes and ears watching our every move."

My brother's voice rang through my head. *Never meet a man unchaperoned.* But John was not here, and it was not as if the duke was a random dandy from the countryside. My thoughts flashed to Danby, but that man was locked up, and I was no longer the naïve, moon-eyed girl I had been back then.

"Alright."

Edmund clasped my gloved hand and led me to the opposite side of the ballroom, away from Anne and Willa. We exited through a side door leading straight outside to a manicured lawn decorated with various topiaries and geometric hedges. The evening air still had a bite to it. It was too early in the season to enjoy the warm summer nights filled with the scent of festive fires and honeysuckle. John and I would heat our sticks of rolled dough over the flames to bake followed by Mrs. Avery's sugary treats and lemonades.

A particularly frosty gale chilled the bare skin on my arms even further. Perhaps this was a bad idea and we should return to the warmth inside.

Next to me, the duke shrugged out of his jacket. "Here," he said, placing it around my shoulders.

I clutched the fabric tighter around my neck. "What about you? Are you not cold, Your Grace?"

"I will be fine. I am warm-blooded." He smirked. "And it is Edmund, remember? We agreed to drop the honorifics."

"Alright," I paused before uttering his name. "Edmund. Why did you want to get me alone?"

His smirk grew wider. "Does a gentleman need a reason to want to be alone with an attractive woman?"

I hid my smile against the collar of his coat. The duke offered me his elbow. Together, we walked the outskirts of the garden. Most of the outdoor area was dark, the only illumination a pale glow coming from the moon above and a brighter golden gleam immediately outside the ballroom windows. If anyone inside was glancing out into the yard, I doubted that they would be able to tell we were there.

Were Anne and Willa wondering what I was doing? I was already dreading Anne's admonishments that would surely follow...

"What are you thinking about?" Edmund asked. "You were frowning just now."

"You could tell?"

He nodded. "Just a slight puckering right there," he lightly pressed his finger between my brows, then brushed the pad of his thumb across the fine feathering of hair. "You look adorable frowning."

"My friends," I stammered, twisting my fingers. "They are probably wondering where I am." I looked up at the duke. "I-We should probably return." His hand finished trailing the side of my face, then he dropped it back to his side. I felt the loss of his touch keenly. How silly to have such strong reactions to a man I barely knew, a man who was never to be mine.

"If you wish," the duke said, still smiling playfully. "Though I must admit that I have enjoyed our walk together. You are not what I expected."

I looked up into his eyes. "What were you expecting?"

"I confess, I was not expecting to find a woman as lovely as you."

I blushed. "No?"

The duke shook his head. "No, but you have beguiled me from the moment I laid my eyes on you. Your fair face framed by that lovely golden hair." He touched one of the ringlets draped in front of my ear. "You are the most beautiful woman at this ball."

He stood so close to me, I held my breath. I wished he would close the remaining distance. But he stopped. "I apologize. You are inexperienced; I should not take advantage of our time alone. We shall have plenty of time to get to know each other."

I sucked in air as my heart sank. Tonight was all the time I would have with the duke. I stared at his handsome face, the proud slant of his lips, and decided I would not be the dutiful sister today. No one could see us from our position, and I assumed that the duke would keep silent whenever he found out who I was. It was unlikely that he wanted to be forced into a marriage with me, so he would keep what I was about to do to himself.

I grasped his shoulder and closed the distance between us. Standing on my toes, I pressed my lips against his. For a moment, he stiffened, his eyes widening at my forwardness, then his lips yielded, and he moved against me. His arm slipped around my waist, lifting me against his body, as our lips moved together and his tongue probed my mouth. I sighed at the sensation of being kissed, his short stubble rubbing against my soft skin, the warmth of his exhales, the musky scent of his skin.

"Lovely," he murmured, nipping at my jaw. "So lovely." My lips throbbed from the pressure of his kisses. His hand roamed the front of my dress, his fingers resting on the swell of my bosom. "My precious Willa."

Hearing the duke whisper Willa's name while his lips caressed my skin stung. None of it was his fault; he was not aware of my identity, but I could not let this progress any further.

I broke our embrace, moving back. "Your Grace—"

"I think Edmund will do fine." He glanced at me, a smile tugging at his lips.

"Edmund." I grasped his hand. "We should return before we are missed."

His gaze flitted to my lips. "Of course, a mhuirnin, it is only our first meeting, after all. There will be plenty of time to seduce you until you agree to marry me." The duke winked. I did my best to hide my expression, smiling warily up at him.

"We shall see if you will succeed," I quipped though I wanted to cry. I was finished with this evening. All I wanted now was to return to my bedroom near Covent Garden.

I slipped off the duke's jacket and pushed it into his hands. "I should probably head in first so the other guests do not see us together."

"And get ideas?" The duke smiled warmly, wagging his brow.

"Indeed." I bit my lip. I was unsure what to say. More than likely I would never see him again. Or if I did, he would be furious about my deception. "Thank you for the dance," I said.

"Perhaps you could save me another, a mhuirnin? The night is not over yet."

"Yes," I told him, though I knew I would fetch Anne and leave as soon as I returned to the ballroom. I turned to him for one last question. "What does that strange word mean?"

His dark eyes gazed at me. "A mhuirnin?"

I nodded.

"It is Gaelic; it means darling."

"Thank you," I whispered. I stood on my tiptoes and pressed one last kiss against his lips. Then I left the duke standing in the dark while I slipped through the side door and back into the crowded ballroom.

Moving through the crowd, I was well aware of my flustered face. I spied Anne across the room pacing together with Willa. As casually as I could, I wound my way back to them. Anne scowled as I neared.

She closed the distance between us and hissed. "Where were you?" Her intelligent brown eyes scoured my face, falling to my lips which no doubt were still swollen from the duke's kisses. Her eyes narrowed further. "What did he do?" Her head moved as she glanced around the room.

"Anne, he is still outside," I said, grabbing her hand. "He did not do anything. I-I will tell you everything when we are alone."

Willa linked her arm with mine and Anne's. "What happened?" she asked. She hushed as she spied the duke's return. "Wait, we should leave the ball first." Anne nodded, agreeing with the redhead. The three of us moved through the gaps in the crowd until we reached the hallway leading back to the foyer.

Lady Westham, speaking with a weak-chinned man and his wife who wore enough feathers in her hair to take flight, blocked the exit. Willa let go of my arm and interrupted our host. "Lady Westham, I want to thank you for your gracious invitation to your ball. It has truly been a splendid evening."

Lady Westham turned away from the weak-chinned man. "Ah, Ms. Balfour, Ms. Easton, and..." she cocked her head towards Anne. "I apologize, I cannot quite remember your name."

"Ms. Blakeley," Anne said with a small curtsy.

"That is right. Are you all off so soon? It is rather early still." Lady Westham's lip curled. "Why, in my time, I would not leave a party until it was well past midnight, sometimes not till dawn."

"I promised father I would not stay out too late," Willa said.

Lady Westham puckered her lips and stared pointedly. "With a duke in attendance who specifically asked for you?"

Willa blushed. "Well, yes. Father wants to ensure that I am well-rested for tomorrow's callers."

"And I suppose it is the same way of it for both of you ladies?" Lady Westham's eyes scanned our faces.

"Yes, Lady Westham," I said while Anne lowered her gaze demurely.

"Be off then." She waved her hand as if chasing off an annoying fly. "I have been known to seek out adventure in my youth once or twice." The elderly woman brushed out of the hallway, her voluminous skirts brushing against ours before she turned her attention to other guests.

At Lady Westham's dismissal we strode purposefully towards the foyer and our exit. Edmund—the duke—would return to the ballroom, finding me, or rather us, missing. A footman opened the front door.

Once outside, Willa grasped my shoulders and pulled me into a hug. "Thank you for playing along."

"You are welcome," I said. "However, I cannot understand why you would not want to meet him. He was…" I blushed. "Perfectly splendid."

Willa's brows rose. "Indeed. Is that why the two of you were away for so long?"

Heat crept up my face, turning my cheeks an even brighter shade of red.

"That is what I thought." Willa chuckled. "Never mind. I am not interested in...that."

Anne shivered next to me. "Is that it then? Are we finished with the charade? I for one am freezing and would like to return to my room."

Willa smiled, snatching a mandarin from a pocket in her skirt. "I suppose so. I only agreed to the one meeting at the dance and that has been fulfilled." She deftly peeled away the outside layer of the fruit and plopped a juicy segment into her mouth. "But promise me," she said, in between bites, "that you will let me take you both out as a thank you." She offered a piece of fruit to Anne who accepted it.

I squeezed Willa's free hand. "Of course, this evening has turned us into friends. You cannot get rid of us now."

6

Harebrained Scheme

I sighed and plopped down on a seat in the hackney cab. Anne scooted in beside me, chewing the segment of mandarin gifted by Willa. My slippered feet ached from standing, and my lips throbbed from the duke's kisses. His musky scent still lingered on my skin.

Had that truly been me initiating our kiss? My ears heated, and I hoped I could escape John's scrutiny when I arrived at the townhouse.

Anne was silent beside me, her hands folded in her lap. I looked at her. From what I could make out in the shadowed cab she looked thin-lipped and annoyed.

"Anne?"

She huffed, unwilling to convey her feelings.

"Are you angry with me?

She sighed. "I need some time to think." We remained quiet the rest of the ride home.

As soon as we entered the house, Anne shot up the stairs to vanish into her own room.

I took a moment to gather myself before I followed her. When I walked into her room, I found Anne sitting on top of the pink bed covers holding a lilac ribbon.

"Mary gave this to me before I left; it is her favorite ribbon." I walked over and joined her on the bed. "She wanted me to have something I could wear to remember her by while I was away."

I glanced at the velvety fabric. "That is sweet of her."

Anne pushed the ribbon beneath her pillow and turned her eyes on me. "Your behavior today was dangerous. I can understand why you went along with Willa's scheme but following the duke outdoors?"

I opened my mouth to speak, but she stopped me.

"Do not tell me that he did not kiss you. I could tell something happened when you returned, and if I could tell what if others noticed as well? Who knows what could have happened to you or your reputation? Do you have a care for any of that?"

I lurched back, her words carving into me as if they were knives. "Of course, I have a care."

Anne frowned and pulled up her legs. "If someone had walked outside and seen you with the duke... The man does not even know who you are, but you could have been forced to marry him."

Anne was right of course; I had been careless, but I did not want to admit it. "I was helping Willa."

Anne sighed, looking entirely displeased with me. "That is what I mean. Why even help Willa? You do not know her. This whole plan was strange from the beginning. Besides, I thought you wanted to attend dances and find your own suitor?"

My cheeks reddened. I thought of my introduction to the Irish duke, his dark eyes boring into me as he brushed his lips against the top of my hand.

"I do," I started.

Anne snorted; it was clear she did not believe me. "You cannot possibly think about the duke. He does not know who you are; his arrangement is with the real Willa."

Her words hit right on target, barbs stinging my heart. It was foolish to think of Edmund and hope for more. I came to London to enjoy being out in public, to dance and wear pretty dresses. I did not set out to find love; I wanted to flirt and have fun.

Perhaps in the future I could find what my brother had with Rose. Or maybe I would find love as William had with Austin. However, I doubted there was a man from the future waiting for me. I could not trust my own instincts when it came to men. Mr. Danby had fooled me into thinking he loved me. What if something like that happened again? I needed certainty or nothing at all.

My mind wandered back to the duke, picturing the proud slant of his mouth, the way his eyes crinkled when he was amused.

"You are right, Anne. I apologize for roping you into this scheme." Her face softened, and she grasped my hand. "No, I apologize. I had no right to chide you as if you were a child. We are friends."

I smiled. "Yes."

She nodded. "I just worry about you...about myself...about

Mary. Sometimes it feels as if all I do is fret. Be careful, that is all I am asking. Follow your heart and marry someone you love or never marry and teach at Rose's school; it does not matter what you choose as long as it is your decision." Anne sounded wistful.

Softly, I asked. "What would you do if you could choose?"

"Strange," Anne snorted softly, her eyes glazed as if she were staring at something in the distance. "No one has ever asked me that before. But that is precisely the problem, isn't it?" Her gaze returned to me, eyes clear and piercing. "We do not have a choice, not really. Not as long as we are treated as property instead of living, breathing human beings. Why is it that men can drink, fight, and gamble? Why are they free to lose entire fortunes when women are the ones who are left with the consequences?"

"Is this about..."

"My brother?" Anne laughed wryly. "Somewhat, I suppose. I love Randolph, I do. But I cannot help that I blame him...and my poor papa." Anne sighed, burying her face in her hands. "Oh, Beth. I hope you do not think me awful."

I laid my hand against Anne's upper back, rubbing in a manner that I hoped would feel comforting. "I would never. You know me, our situations are not the same; however, that does not stop me from understanding."

After all, most women were in a similar situation; I was just lucky that John was my brother. It could have been worse, even if he was a bit overprotective.

Anne nodded, rubbing her eyes before dropping her hands in her lap. "I wish I had a choice. There is so much I would do different." She smiled up at me. "I know you have been eager to join the London season. You always wanted to attend and be a part of the excitement. But I...I never wanted that. Being a wife has never been something I looked forward to, though it has been the only thing I have been expected to do."

My heart ached for my friend. I wanted to help her, but I did not know how.

"I want to travel and receive an education as Randolph did," Anne continued. "Why can't I read history books and study science? I want to travel Europe, see the Alps, swim in the Mediterranean." Anne slumped forward. "Though it can never be."

"Perhaps we can inquire at different schools."

Anne shook her head. "Even if they accept a woman, with what money? My mother, Randolph, and Mary all rely on my making a good match. My mother in particular has been getting more and more desperate after each failed season." Anne kicked at the floorboards, scuffing the heel of her slippers against the wood. "It hardly matters. Once a suitor finds out I have no dowry, they all bow out to hunt for a better prospect. The silliest thing is that even though I do not want to be married the rejections still sting." Anne's shoulders slumped.

"I do not want to marry yet either."

"What?" A pair of red-rimmed eyes glanced up at me. "Then why were you so insistent on joining the season?"

I snorted. "I said I do not yet want to marry, not that I do not want to dance and flirt and attend parties."

"But I remember you used to talk about marriage and finding someone to love."

"I did..." I let out a deep sigh. "Do you remember Mr. Danby?"

"What does he have to do with anything?"

"Hardly anyone knows this but when Mr. Danby was staying in Westbridge he started courting me in secret. He spoke of being in love with me and getting married whenever we met in secret, which was as often as I could get away from John's watchful eye. My brother seemed to dislike him when he was in attendance during social events, but I was blinded by Mr. Danby's words and had fashioned myself equally as in love. We had made a plan to elope."

"Beth—"

"I was a fool, a lucky fool. John and Rose managed to catch up to us in time and foil Mr. Danby's plan. By then he had already shed his mask. Every word he uttered to me had been a lie; he was only interested in my dowry. I was not even the only woman he duped."

"How has no one heard of this?"

"John and William made sure to silence him and send him off with a constable so my honor would remain intact."

Anne chewed her lip, understanding in her eyes. "What happened wasn't your fault. Though I can understand why John has been so insistent on having a chaperon."

"Not my fault? I trusted him and lied to my brother and to Rose. I never once considered he might not be telling the truth. Was I not wrong for meeting him in secret, for agreeing to elope?"

Anne shook her head. "You think the best of people. It is his fault for not living up to it."

"You can say it. You can call me naive. That day, the day of our elopement...I was a bit nervous, but overall, I was excited. I thought I was set to marry the man I loved, but as soon as we left his demeanor changed. The turn was so sudden and jarring it was as if he had slapped me across the face. Gone was his smile and warm voice, his eyes cold as he ordered me to sit down and stay quiet. That's when I knew I had made a huge mistake."

"He was just one awful man. That does not mean that you are naive or that you could not find someone honest and true."

"How would I know? What if I listen to pretty lies and empty promises and believe another impostor like that?"

Anne shook her head. "Is that why you went along with Willa's hair-brained scheme? Because as long as you are pretending, it is safe? You can dance and flirt with the knowledge that it could never turn into something more?"

My cheeks reddened. Her point had shot straight through my core. "There is nothing more to it. This was a one-time occurrence; I shall never meet the duke again. Besides, I made the deal with Willa while thinking of you. She agreed to invite us along to dances that host the ton and, if you still want to make a match that is, help find you eligible bachelors."

Anne appeared taken aback. "She will?"

"Yes, so this harebrained scheme, as you put it, might be of some use after all."

7

Invitation to Bambreich Manor

"Anne, Beth, are you coming down?" Rose's voice traveled up the stairs, pulling me from my slumber.

I covered my ears with the pillow and groaned. Last night, Anne and I had stayed up late, with our conversation ending long past our early departure from Mrs. Westham's ball. The effects of which became evident this morning; my head throbbed with an annoying banging at my temples, and my eyelids were heavy and did not want to open. I opened my mouth which was also uncomfortably dry and yawned, stretching my arms above my head.

Rose shouted something more. "You should see what has arrived."

I groaned again and kicked off the bedspread. Slowly, I sat up and wiggled my toes. Feeling worse for wear, I crossed the room and examined my face in the vanity mirror. Thankfully, a full pitcher of crisp water stood ready next to the washing basin. I filled the bowl and splashed the cool water on my splotchy face. I swiped my crusted eyes and forced myself to wake up.

Someone rapped against my door. "Ready, miss?" Estelle called from the hallway.

"You can come in." I patted my face dry with a hand towel.

Estelle barreled in and, efficient as always, pulled a few of dresses from the wardrobe. "Which would you like to wear today? Might I recommend the pale purple."

I glanced at the simple muslin dress she was holding up. "That will do."

A scullery maid entered to retrieve my bedpan while I took off my nightgown. I sat down at the edge of the bed and pulled on new white stockings. Estelle handed me a fresh chemise. I stood so she could help me adjust the knee-length chemise and fasten my stays. She fastened the hooks on the stays and pulled down the neckline of the chemise so they would not peek out from underneath the dress.

Once we finished putting on my undergarments, Estelle lowered the purple dress over my head, fastened the matching ribbon in the back, and straightened the gauze bow under-lining my bust.

Estelle and I were used to each other which in turn meant we moved through every step of dressing with ease. I lowered myself to my vanity seat while my ladies' maid picked up a brush from the table. She tugged on my hair as she worked the brush through a few tangles. Before I knew it, she had fin-ished combing and fastened my hair into an easy day style.

"Thank you," I told her before heading downstairs.

Something floral tinged the air when I reached the landing. I knew what had arrived before I even reached the bottom of the staircase. A maid was primping several bouquets, placing them into vases to be displayed along the hallway.

"Are those for us?" Anne said from behind me.

Rose nodded, an amused smile playing along her lips. "It seems you both made an impression last night." She walked to the first bouquet. "This one is for Anne from a Mr. Cosgrove."

"I wonder if Mr. Cosgrove is the man I danced with," Anne said.

I skipped down the last few treads and joined Rose. "Could be. What's this one?" I pulled out the card. "Mr. Fillmore...I suppose he must have been either the sandy-haired man in the blue brocade vest or the one with the broad shoulders in shiny top boots." I turned to Rose. "Does that mean they want to come call on us soon?"

"Most likely," John said from the doorway. He leaned against the frame and lifted his brow. "Preferable during a time which I can be present."

"Why would you need to be present? Anne and I are more than capable of—"

"I am aware of what you are capable of. This is still my household, so I am going to be present to vet any of the men." He picked at a flower from the nearest vase.

"Or chase them away," I grumbled.

"Regardless, I shall be the one to oversee any meetings," John continued. "Now, how about we make our way to the dining room. We can discuss matters further while we break our fast."

Rose grabbed something from the sideboard. "Before I forget, this also arrived for you, Beth." Rose pressed a letter into my hands.

I turned it over in my hands, noting the B stamped into the wax seal. Could this be from Willa? Her father was the marquis of Bambreich, after all. Rose followed John, leaving us alone in the foyer.

Anne came to the same conclusion because she nudged me and said, "Go on, let us see what she wants."

Tearing open the paper, I flipped the letter and began reading Willa's message.

Dear Beth,

I am sending this letter to ask if you could meet me today at Bambreich Manor. Please come as soon as you are able and bring your friend. I will tell you the details in person.

Signed your friend,
Willa Balfour

"Huh, Willa wants us to visit her today as soon as we are able."

"She does? I wonder what for." Anne chewed the corner of her lip. "I mean...the ruse is over, is it not?"

"I was under that impression, yes." My heart lurched. Last night had been exhilarating. I'd never felt that kind of pull towards someone before, not even when I fashioned myself in love with Mr. Danby. But the scheme had ended, and that was for the best.

"We should go, should we not? Find out what Willa wants. Are you sure she did not mention anything in her letter? Not a single clue?"

I shook my head and handed her the letter. "No, you can see for yourself." Anne read the short letter and frowned. I turned on my heel. "I'll let John know."

John and Rose sat at the dining room table, taking sips of tea.

John glanced up from his plate. "Eat some berries."

"Berries this early?" What a treat. I popped one of the purplish clusters into my mouth, tartness flooding my mouth. "Why not sit down?" John said, smirking.

"I do not have time. The letter I received was from Willa Balfour, the daughter of the Marquis of Bambreich. We met at the modiste and again last night. She invited Anne and me to her home."

John swallowed a berry. "I can send word for the driver to be ready, but surely you and Anne can take the time to eat first."

I understood John's point, but I was also excited to go.

John lifted his brow. "Beth..."

"Alright, I shall break my fast before leaving." I raised my voice towards the hallway. "Anne, come try these berries."

John stood and pulled a cord hanging from the wall. A few minutes later, the butler entered.

"You rang, sir?"

"Thank you, Bartley. Could you alert the driver that Ms.

Blakeley and my sister will need the carriage to visit a friend? Ask Tom to ready it for departure soon."

***

About an hour later, Anne and I faced Willa in the midst of a spacious sitting room.

"What was so urgent? Is it something to do with the duke?" I asked Willa.

"Shh." Willa's eyes flitted to the doorway. "Not yet."

I glanced behind me, but there was no one there. Even the butler who escorted us inside had left.

I turned back to Willa. "Wha—"

"Hello, Papa," Willa cut me off. She smiled wide as she sidestepped me and greeted an older man with graying sideburns. Aside from the sideburns, he still had a full head of dark hair; his physique was wiry not yet soft around the middle like many other middle-aged men.

"Let me introduce you to my friends, Ms. Blakeley and Ms. Easton."

"It is always wonderful to meet any of my daughter's friends," Lord Balfour said. "Where did you three meet?"

"The modiste," Anne said.

The Marquis of Bambreich let out a small snort. "The modiste, eh? Perhaps I need to beseech the two of you to change my daughter's mind about wearing new dresses."

"I have dresses aplenty, Papa."

"I hope you do not mean the orange monstrosity you wore last night." Willa's cheeks turned red. "That is what I thought." Willa's father sighed. "Sweetheart, please do your father one favor. You look so much like your late mother I would like nothing more than to see you dressed in one of her favorite colors."

"I shall consider it."

Willa's father nodded. "That is all I ask." He scraped his throat and smiled at Anne and me. "Well, I shall return to my study and leave you girls to your own devices. Perhaps I will meet you both later if you stay long enough for cream tea."

"I shall make sure they will," Willa said. She waited until her father had left and closed the double doors behind her, resting her back against the light wood.

"Your father is sweet," Anne said.

"My papa is." Willa shrugged, turning her ear towards the door. She paused briefly. "However, I feel like he is pushing me away. Perhaps I remind him too much of my mother."

"She must have been very special. I am sorry for your loss," Anne said.

"Thank you." Willa sighed. "It has been a few years, but Papa is still in mourning. He has hardly left the house since she died; I worry about him."

Anne nodded. "My father passed away two years ago. My mother has not even set foot in his study yet. It is still exactly as he left it, cluttered with his things."

Willa sighed as she stepped away from the doors and meandered through the room. "I think my father is trying to arrange a marriage for me to assure himself that I will not be left alone." Her face sunk as she said it. "I do not know why he feels the need to arrange that. He is not going anywhere, and I like my life as it is." A soft, sad chuckle crossed Willa's lips. "Let us change the subject; we do not need to speak about my father. I invited you for a reason, after all."

"Yes, I was wondering about that," I said. "Does it have to do with last night?"

"It does, and I apologize for shushing you earlier. I did not want my papa to overhear."

"What is it?" Anne asked.

"It appears the duke enjoyed his evening with you, Beth." Willa quirked her brow.

"Uhm, he should not have?"

Willa stared deadpan at me. "Since he is under the impression that you are me, and I have no intention of getting married, no. It would have been better if he had disliked his interaction with you." She threw up her hands. "But what is done is done. However, I received a letter stating that he is coming to visit me and my father here tomorrow." She snorted. "And my father cannot find out about our arrangement."

I frowned and took a seat in one of the chairs. "What do you propose we should do?"

"I have not thought that far ahead."

"Is your father aware that the duke is coming here?" Anne asked.

"No, I managed to sneak it out of the pile of letters."

I tapped my finger against my bottom lip. "What if you managed to get him out of the house, keep your father busy somewhere? I could take your place in this room?"

Anne frowned. "Willa, can you not send the duke a note and cancel?"

Willa hummed. "What if he still turns up or does not accept my cancellation? He could take it upon himself to visit my father and me regardless."

Anne folded her arms, her expression every bit that of a chaperon. "It is a risky plan; anything could go wrong. What about the staff?"

"Let me fret about that." Willa continued pacing. "I might be able to send them along with Papa. Perhaps leave one scullery maid for serving tea."

"What if the scullery maid tells anyone? And how do you plan to lure your father out of the house?" Anne shook her head. "I do not think this plan is going to work."

"Is it not easier to stop our ruse now?" I crossed my legs. "We cannot keep this ruse going. What if the duke wants more visits?"

Willa clasped my hands. "Please, Beth. I cannot do this without you. Will you please help do this? I assure you I will keep my promise."

Anne rolled her eyes. "Is that the promise where you will find me a good match?"

Willa's eyes widened, and she bobbed her head. "Yes, I will make sure."

Anne's gaze flitted between me and Willa, a hand on her hip. "I thank you but I do not need assistance with finding a husband."

Willa sized Anne up. I could almost hear her brain whirring as she thought of what to say next. Anne stared back at Willa, her pointed chin raised, a proud slant to her lips. It had been a while since I had seen Anne's confidence.

Breaking first, Willa said, "Alright. Perhaps instead we can continue our friendship *sans* matchmaking. If that is amenable to you?"

Anne quirked her lips. "Perhaps."

"So, what happens if I accept?" I said, breaking up the tension between them.

Willa broke her eyes away from Anne. She started ticking off items on her fingers. "Step one; I will need to find a way to lure my papa away from the house. Step two; you need to be here ready to pretend to be me. Step three; you need to dissuade the duke from wanting any future visits. Preferably you get him to revoke his intentions of marriage."

I scratched the back of my neck. "Because that sounds easy enough..." Willa caught my sarcasm and stopped pacing.

"His letter stated that he will be here around eleven. Will you be able to arrive before then?"

John and Rose would not mind me leaving early to visit a friend. "I believe so."

The door to the sitting room opened, and the butler appeared.

"Ms. Balfour, another visitor arrived for you."

A small frown line appeared between Willa's brows. "Another visitor? I wasn't expecting anyone."

"Said the name was a Ms. Melinda."

Melinda...the name sounded familiar. Where had I heard it before? I racked my brain for a moment before I remembered and nearly gasped. Wasn't that the name of the time-traveling bookshop lady?

"Middle-aged, curly brown hair?" I asked Willa's butler.

He nodded while Willa asked, "You know the visitor?"

"I might." Though if she was who I thought she was, I wondered why she would show up at this place and time.

"You can show her in," Willa said.

The butler nodded and retreated. He returned a minute

later, followed by a curvy woman, bouncy curls framing her face. She wore a maroon dress that suited her well.

Melinda smiled and strode toward me. "Beth, it has been a while." She turned and nodded to Anne and Willa. "And these must be your friends."

Willa lifted her brow, her gaze flitting between Melinda and myself. "It is a pleasure to meet one of Beth's acquaintances, but how did you know to find her here?"

Before Melinda could answer, I grabbed her sleeve and pulled her away.

"Please excuse us for a moment," I told Willa as I exited the room. I lowered my voice and focused on the bookshop lady. "Why are you here?"

"Are you not pleased to see me?"

I spluttered. "No. Is it William? Did something happen?" My mind raced. "Wait, it isn't Rose? She cannot leave; it would break my brother's heart."

Melinda chuckled. "Calm down, it is none of that. Last I checked, William and Austin were very happy. In fact, they were visiting Rose's parents."

"Oh." I breathed in and out. "Then why are you here?"

"I would like to ask you the same."

"Me? What do I have to do with anything?" Melinda shrugged. "My bookshop decided I needed to be here. I'm not sure why myself."

"I thought that you..."

Melinda shook her head and chuckled. "It doesn't work exactly like that. Well, I can choose to go places and times but the bookshop is... intuitive. Yes, that's the right word."

"Intuitive?"

"It senses what a person might need and will take them there."

"So, it took Rose to John and Austin to William."

"That is the gist of it."

"Then why are you here now?"

Melinda scrutinized my face. I took a step back and bumped into the wall. Her stare unnerved me.

"We should return to—"

"Has anything unusual happened to you?" Melinda asked, cutting off my nervous mumbling.

I shook my head before adding, "Well..."

"Well?" Melinda waited for me to continue.

"Willa—the redheaded woman—asked me to switch identities."

Melinda muttered something under her breath. I swore I heard the words "just like" and "movie".

She grinned. "Why does Willa need you to switch identities?"

I hesitated. "Her father wants to marry her off to an Irish duke; however, she does not want to marry anyone. She has asked me to take her place and dissuade the duke."

Something I could not quite define glinted in Melinda's eyes. She nodded sagely. "I see."

Confused, I said, "See what?"

Willa's head popped out. "Everything alright?"

"Yes," Melinda said. "Beth here filled me in on everything."

"I did?" I said at the same time that Willa uttered, "She has?"

Willa shot me an accusing glare.

"Don't worry, I'm here to help." Melinda flashed a reassuring smile.

This seemed to mollify Willa, and she let out a puff of air. "We should continue discussing our plan in the sitting room then. My father will return soon for cream tea, and he cannot find out."

8

Commence The Charade

After discussing our plan the evening before, I arrived at Bambreich mansion early in the morning. Willa popped out of the back door whispering my name. I stood huddled near the tall rhododendron bushes decorating the wall; the delicate lavender blooms seemed like the appropriate place to hide my presence.

"Here," I said. My stomach coiled, making it hard to keep my composure.

"Are you ready?" Willa fidgeted with the sleeve of her jacket. She appeared nervous as I met her near the servants' entrance. "No one has seen you?"

I pulled back the hood of my cape and shook my head. "I do not believe so. Anne and Melinda are waiting outside of the gate to give us a few minutes before they knock on the door. Hopefully you will all have a good time at the circus while I entertain the duke."

"Hopefully it will be a long time." Willa worried her lip and peered around the garden. Once she was satisfied there was no one there, she said, "Alright, Suzie is waiting for us in the servants' quarter. She will keep you company until we have left."

She led me inside, past the kitchen, and into a plain hallway. "We have got to hurry; my father might come looking for me."

I kept quiet as she rushed us past multiple closed doors until she stopped so suddenly, I nearly bumped into her.

She knocked on one of the doors, a quick rasp of knuckles before the door opened and revealed a young woman. Light wisps of hair were visible beneath a baby blue cap.

"Ms. Willa," she said, opening the door further and waving us in. Her head popped around the corner to check the hallway before closing her door.

I smiled at the scullery maid. "My name is Beth Easton."

"Nice to meet you Ms. Easton." The maid stood stiffly, awkward at being cramped in her small bedroom with two other women. "You can take the chair." She pointed at a single simple chair that stood next to a half table. I nodded, shuffling past Willa, and took a seat.

The room was sparse; a pallet for sleeping pressed against the wall, a desk standing opposite, and the single chair I now used. The only things that made the drab room more personable were a few of the maid's personal affects. A tattered copy of *Evelina* on the pillow, a stack of clothing perched on the desk, and a copper locket hanging from a nail in the wall.

"Will you manage, Suzie?" Willa said.

The girl bobbed her head. "Yes, miss. I'll be right as rain."

"Alright. Just make sure to refer to Ms. Easton as Ms. Balfour. I shall try to keep Papa occupied until supper."

Willa turned to me. "Good luck and please try to get rid of the duke this time."

"I will try," I said with more confidence than I felt.

"Let us commence the charade." Willa inhaled deep and slow to gather herself and left the room. Her voice traveled down the hall as she called for her father.

"And now we wait," I muttered to myself. Suzie took a seat on her pallet. She tapped her fingers against her thighs, making awkward glances around the room.

"Do you like it here?" I asked.

"Hmm?" she said, swiveling her face towards me.

"Do you enjoy working for Willa and her father?"

"Very much." The girl smiled. "Ms. Willa and her father are kindhearted employers."

"How long have you worked for them?"

"They hired me as maid of all trades when I was twelve." Suzie thought for a moment. "So, it's been about five years."

"That is a long time."

Suzie nodded. "But they are fair and let me work my way up. I'm a housemaid now," she added with a hint of pride.

"That is wonderful," I agreed.

Suzie and I waited in her room until all the noise had quieted and until we were certain that the Marquis of Bambreich's household had left. Then she stood and peeked out of her door.

"Ms. Willa," she hollered out for good measure before giving me a determined nod. I followed her from the servants' quarter into the foyer.

"Why are you doing this?" I asked. "It is risky, and Lord Balfour might not look kindly upon the part you have played if we are found out."

A pair of bright blue eyes glanced up at me. "Ms. Willa has always been kind to me." Suzie's cheeks flushed pink. "I consider her my friend, miss."

Friends with a maid. The thought made me smile as well as raise my opinion of Willa. I considered my ladies maid Estelle a friend as well though friendships with staff members tended to be a rarity. Many other wealthier landowners and members of the ton considered fraternizing with the staff as beneath them.

John and I never shared those views. Perhaps it was our upbringing. From what I remembered, my parents were kind and generous employers. They included the staff in our holidays, made sure they were well-fed and clothed, and ensured that they had time to themselves.

Of course, after my parents passed away, Mrs. Avery had stepped up and taken on the role of mother hen. We were still trying to piece our lives back together then. Mrs. Avery was there to support us as my brother became head of the household and had no qualms about talking sense into him when he needed it.

No, Mrs. Avery was not staff, she was family. And so were the others.

"Miss, we should see you settled in the sitting room. The duke will be here any moment now." Suzie threw open the double doors and ushered me into the comfortable room.

The previous day I had taken a seat in a green tufted chair, but then I had been a guest. Now, I needed to take on the role of Lady Willa Balfour.

I bypassed the chair and planted myself on the settee. The entire room was visible from this angle. My stomach turned, and I could not help but tap my foot as I tried to throw off my nerves.

The duke was expecting a lady and that was who I needed to be. However, I was still unsure how I should turn him away from marriage. What could I do?

Tap Tap Tap

I locked eyes with Suzie. She nodded once before striding towards the front door. I held my breath. Heavy steps followed Suzie's lighter ones, and before I knew it, the duke stood in front of me. He bowed, and my heart fluttered at the sight of him clad in a tailored jacket and a pair of well-fitting pantaloons. His outfit emphasized every inch of his formidable figure.

"Ms. Balfour," he said once he straightened. His Irish lilt turned everything he said into music.

"Welcome, Your Grace." I stood, flashing a smile.

"Call me Edmund." He smirked. "We have met before, after all. No need to keep up with all the formalities."

I inclined my head. "Indeed." I pointed towards the chairs. "Please, make yourself comfortable."

Edmund adjusted his jacket and took a seat opposite me.

Suzie flitted to our sides. "Would Your Grace like a cup of tea?"

"Yes, thank you." Suzie looked to me, and I nodded my head.

"Where is the rest of the staff?" Edmund asked once Suzie left the room.

"My papa is away for the day and brought most of the staff along with him."

"So, I have you all to myself. How scandalous." The duke's lips raised into a teasing smile.

My skin prickled. The invitation behind his words was clear. My mouth went dry, and I became aware of how private the room was."

"We could take a walk," I hurried to say.

"Perhaps a tour of your home is in order?" Edmund suggested.

"Perhaps..." But it wasn't my home, I had no real grasp of the layout. If I took Edmund on a tour of Willa's home, it would become clear to even the most gullible person that I had no clue where I was going. And then there was our forced proximity walking through the corridors. I swallowed thickly. No, I could not do that.

"Actually," I said. "I am feeling a bit overheated. I would rather take advantage of the cooler weather today and take a stroll through our garden. Did you notice the rhododendron bushes upon arrival?"

"Whatever you wish, my lady," the duke said. "Perhaps you can give a tour of the house at a later time."

We bumped into Suzie in the foyer; she was carrying a silver tray with cups of tea and a small platter of biscuits.

"Thank you, Suzie," I said. My mouth was drier than the Sahara Desert, so I picked up a cup and took a quick swig of tea, the warm liquid soothing my throat. "You can leave the tea for now. The duke and I are going to take a stroll outside."

"Yes, miss." The duke glanced back at Suzie while I ushered him out the front door. His puzzled expression showed his confusion at my insistence on heading out that moment, especially when there was fresh brewed tea to be had.

I wanted to sigh. Willa had asked one thing of me; to get the duke to no longer want to marry me. Therefore, I needed to change up the way I was acting. I had been too polite. How would I make the duke withdraw his intentions of marriage?

Flashes of Mrs. Brocklehurst came to mind. No one liked a braggart. I needed to pretend to be someone else, someone that would make a man like the duke run far away.

I scraped my throat and puffed out my chest as if I was a peacock parading around. "We have got the finest garden in London," I boasted. "My papa hires the best landscapers from all over England each season." I made sure to make my voice sound lofty.

Edmund slid past me, his hand skimming mine. "And these are the rhododendrons you mentioned? Your landscapers must be talented to produce such lovely flowers." His eyes met mine. "Almost as lovely as you."

My heart thumped. But I could not forget myself and bungle my mission. I burst out into an obnoxious giggle. "You are such a flatterer."

From that point on, I made sure to giggle at every single thing the duke said. I did not know how he kept his composure. If someone was giggling like that near me, I would have told them off from the start, but here Edmund was, as charming as he had been at the ball.

We took a turn past a patch of hyacinths when the duke asked," What is your opinion of marriage?"

"As long as the income of my suitor is enough to keep me dressed in the latest fashion then I have no objections. However, I cannot go without jewelry and new dancing slippers and new gowns at least every quarter. I will also need plenty of staff to accommodate any parties I will be hosting." I pulled my lips into a sweet smile. "I am certain you want your wife to be the center of attention."

The duke needed to go. I mulled over the little information I had heard about him. Most of it was gossip; therefore, one might wonder how much of it was truth. Nevertheless, everyone I had heard speak about the duke mentioned how rarely the duke made an appearance in London. That must mean the duke liked living in Ireland.

Edmund might have the makings of a fine family man, preferring a quiet life in the countryside, overseeing his tenants, hunting and taking pleasure rides on his estate, doting on his future wife. However, Willa wanted him gone...and I had no place in his life either.

I lifted my chin, the soft breeze ruffling my dress. "I will need you to leave your estate in Ireland behind for London, of course. There is no possibility of me leaving my papa or the London society behind. I am too fond of the parties here." I showed off my teeth. "I am amenable to living with my father or at your London home. Which do you prefer?"

I detected a hint of terror in his expression, my words were having an effect. I had to stifle a grin.

"I shall need to inspect your London home before you make a decision," I continued. "When shall we go?"

"Not yet," Edmund said. He continued striding along the garden path with his arms clasped behind his back. "We should get to know each other more first before we make any hasty decision."

"It is not hasty if you have agreed to my father's proposition."

"Ah, yes," the duke chuckled. "I suppose. But I would like to ascertain whether we will be a suitable match. Would you not like to be certain as well?"

I smiled bright. "You are a duke, what more is there?"

Edmund frowned. "You would marry me even if we had nothing in common? What about our conversation during the night we met?"

"I changed my mind."

"You can change your mind that quickly?"

"For a duke... always. And we will have the rest of our lives together for you to grow to enjoy what I enjoy."

"Dresses and parties."

"In London, yes. And don't forget the jewelry and slippers." I giggled once more.

"I see." The duke paused at a Roman bust.

"Yes?" I added. I pushed myself against him. He had withdrawn more and more during the length of our conversation; there was no chance the duke wanted to continue a marriage with me. Perhaps he was trying to find the words to end our courtship. I felt awful for the way I treated him, but I accomplished the promise I made to Willa. She would be free of him, and I would return to enjoy society as myself.

Edmund bent and picked a narcissus from the garden. Lowering his head, he smelled the yellow flower before turning to me. He reached out, tucking the flower behind my ear. His hand brushed along my cheek on its way down. I reddened at his touch, the roughness of his thumb against my soft flesh setting my skin aflame. Why did this man have such a strong effect on me?

"Lovely," he said, confusing my feelings further. How was it possible that the duke was still interested in me? Had the man no sense at all?

"Ms. Balfour, would you do me the honor of accompanying me to Covent Garden, tomorrow?"

"Tomorrow?"

"I can arrange for my driver to pick you up?"

What was I supposed to do? I had no reason to decline. Willa had to understand.

"I shall await your carriage," I told the duke.

"I look forward to getting to know you better," Edmund said. "Perhaps I'll get to meet the Marquis of Bambreich and receive a tour of your home next time I visit."

"Perhaps."

I managed to say my goodbyes to the duke before Willa and her father returned.

"Did it work?" Suzie asked when I came indoors.

"I tried my best. You would not believe how awful I was. But he still wants to see me again."

Suzie's eyes widened. "Oh no. Willa was hoping for this to be over."

I pursed my lips. "I am sorry that I failed. The duke paid no attention to any of my peculiar behavior. Instead, he invited me to go to Covent Garden with him tomorrow."

Suzie sighed. "It isn't your fault. How about I make us a fresh pot of tea and we retreat to my room to wait for Willa?"

"What about the tea from earlier?"

"Already disposed of. There is no trace left of anyone having been in the sitting room." Suzie shuffled off towards the kitchen.

9

Covent Garden

There I was, seated next to Edmund Humphries, on my way to Covent Garden. Anne was taking the roll of chaperon very serious, glowering at the both of us at every possible turn. Both she and Willa had impressed upon me the need to end the courtship.

"It will not end well for either of us," Willa had said when she returned home and found me waiting in Suzie's room. I had quickly filled her in on everything that happened. "This dalliance with the duke needs to end." She had frowned and folded her arms in front of her. "Are you certain you were chasing him away?"

"I was."

"Then why would he continue to court you?" She had raised her brow as she swept her gaze along my body. "Is he that shallow?"

I scoffed at her. "I suppose there was a compliment in there somewhere, but there is no need to be rude."

Willa had seemed suitably ashamed. "I apologize, I had just hoped he would cut ties with me and run back to Ireland."

I pulled her in for a hug. "I really did try."

"I know. Thank you."

The carriage wobbled along the cobblestone streets while I avoided Anne's gaze and focused my attention on the duke. "What do you have planned at Covent Garden?"

"You shall find out," he said. "I am certain you will enjoy it."

The duke's driver dropped us off at the edge of a bustling square. An array of stalls stood at the center, some nothing more than a slab of wood holding produce, while other structures and covered buildings sprawled out across the area. Everywhere I turned there were people; small urchins in rags, members of the ton strolling about in their fineries, merchants shouting out their wares, and everything in between. A well-dressed couple passed us by, the woman holding up a parasol to protect herself from the sun.

"Where to first?" I asked. Edmund held out his hand as if he wanted me to take it and run away with him into the crowd. But a disapproving glance from Anne made him retract his hand just as fast.

"Ahum," he said, scratching his throat. "What do you ladies think about coffee?"

"I cannot say that I have tasted it before. My..." I halted. I had been about to say my brother. "My papa prefers Imperial tea to coffee."

"This should be a treat then," the duke said. "If you ladies will follow me." He glanced back at Anne and me while opening up a path through the crowd, making sure we kept pace with him and would not get lost in the crowd.

Edmund stopped in front of a squat building. The outside was rather nondescript, but inside, through the open doors, I could see heavy yellow wallpapering and a bar lined with many drink accouterments. Many men lined the bar, and mixed groups sat at tables. Birds of paradise, women wearing bright frocks and fluffy plumes in their hair, circled groups of men, smiling coquettishly.

My eyes widened at the sight of them. With my brother usually taking his role of protector rather seriously, I had never seen women like them. It was fascinating.

"We cannot go inside there," Anne said, her voice shrill. She shot an accusing glare at the duke.

"We are not, I assure you."

A couple of round tables stood propped in a corner outside the coffee house, shaded by an overhang. Edmund found an empty one and directed us to take a seat. I sneaked a last glance at the women inside before tearing my eyes away and sitting down at the table.

"Wait for me. I will be only a moment," the duke said.

"Why would the duke take us to such a place?" Anne said once he left.

"I like it." I glanced around at the crowds passing by. "John would never let me visit a place like this. I'm no longer a child, and I do not need to be protected from normal life."

"I never said that."

"No, but you sure are acting like a dour old matron and not my friend.

Anne harrumphed. I bent towards her and lowered my voice.

"Is the reason for your sour mood perhaps the absence of a certain redheaded daughter of a marquis?"

"No," Anne spluttered.

"Mmm, so you would not rather spend the afternoon with her?"

"I am not certain what you are trying to insinuate," Anne scoffed.

"Nothing at all," I said before Anne could get worked up even more.

"Perhaps we should focus on the duke, and how you are going to get rid of him."

"I suppose."

Anne nodded.

"But then we would no longer have a reason to meet with Willa," I added.

"I see what you are doing." Anne's eyes narrowed. "You are deflecting your feelings for the duke onto me." She sighed, her voice softening. Anne's hand slid across the table until she gripped mine. "It does not matter whether you like him. He does not know the real you. I apologize if it is difficult to hear."

I returned the squeeze, her hand comfortable in mine. "No, you are telling me the truth. I do need to end it even if a part of me does not want to. You have seen him; he's...wonderful."

"And not for you. There can be no future between you."

"What are you ladies discussing?"

I dropped Anne's hand and scooted back into my seat, looking up at the handsome dark-haired man.

The duke stood smiling with his arms behind his back. With a graceful swing he pulled his hands forward, presenting us with two bouquets of daffodils.

A waiter arrived, dropping off three cups of coffee while Edmund presented them to us. A nutty almost buttery scent wafted from the dark liquid in front of me. I accepted the daffodils and laid them beside me.

"Before we enjoy the coffee, I have one more surprise." Edmund pulled something from his pocket; a handkerchief fastened around bulbous forms. He laid his handkerchief on the table and untied it, revealing small, red fruits.

"Strawberries, this early?" Anne appeared delighted.

The duke nodded. "I spotted them at a stall as we made our way through the crowd. The seller said they were the first crop from a nearby hothouse. Please, eat some."

I wasted no time and grabbed one of the plump fruits. Slightly tart, but delicious sweetness flooded my taste buds.

"Thank you for sharing."

The three of us finished the handful of berries fast enough for the coffee to have cooled to the perfect temperature. I washed the fruit down with the bitter drink.

So far, Edmund had been the perfect companion. So much so that even Anne was not able to keep a scowl on her face.

"If you ladies are all finished, let us take a stroll around the market," the duke suggested.

Once we stood, Edmund offered us his arm. I hooked my arm with his, reveling in the firmness of his muscles against my own while I held the bouquet of daffodils in the crook of my other arm. Together, we pushed back into the fray.

"Ms. Blakeley, you must have some wonderful stories to tell about Ms. Balfour," the duke said as we stopped at a display of hats and brooches. Massive plumes, feathers, and faux flowers stuck out from all manner of hats. I even saw a straw hat adorned with fake strawberries as lush as the ones I had just eaten.

"I couldn't possibly," Anne said.

"Oh, you must entertain me with a story. How did you two meet?"

I unhooked my arm and picked up one of the straw caps, touching the soft pink ribbon adorning it.

"It is nothing interesting," I told the duke as I glanced back at him. "We have known each other since we were children."

"Is that right?" The duke grabbed the hat from my hands and placed it gently upon my head. Then, taking the two ends of ribbon, fastened it into a bow beneath my chin. I could see his throat bob as his eyes fastened on mine. His thumb caressed the slope of my neck as he let go of the ribbon. My heart fluttered much too fast for my liking. For a moment, the whole world fell away, and I could have sworn the duke and I were the only two people around. But before I knew it, his hand lifted, and that delicious, intimate heat trailing down my neck dissipated. The world around us flooded back; the thump, thump of the cart wheels, chattering of the people walking the market, clinking of glasses from inside the coffee house.

My breath hitched and my cheeks burned while I searched for words. The duke realized the effect he had on me because his lips raised into a teasing smirk.

"Lovely," he said in a deep, low voice, his dark eyes smoldering, before turning to Anne. "What was Ms. Balfour like as a child?"

"Oh. Ehm." Anne seemed pained. Lying was not her strong suit.

"I loved dresses and dancing as well as riding my pony around the estate." I was about to untie the ribbon when Edmund stopped my hand.

"Keep it. The hat suits you and I would like you to have a reminder of me."

I blushed and let go of the ribbons. "Thank you."

"How about you, Ms. Blakeley? Have any of these hats or accessories caught your attention?"

The three of us moved on from the hat stall with me wearing a straw hat and Anne with a brooch adorning the lapel on her jacket. I enjoyed strolling around Covent Garden with the duke, checking out the wares.

We walked past a young street urchin, a thin girl in rags holding up an empty cup, when I spotted a familiar figure. A tall blonde man with eyes as blue as mine. I stiffened.

John, my brother.

Next to him was Rose having an animated conversation. They had not spotted us, yet, but merely three stalls separated us. I grasped Anne's hand.

"My brother is here," I hissed.

Her eyes widened. "What should we do?"

What should we do indeed? I was in a lot of trouble if my brother spotted me. My breathing picked up speed; I wanted to crawl into a hole and disappear, but I had to remain calm and think. If John found out what I was doing he would send me back to Hawthorne and never let me out of his sight again. I could wave goodbye to society and to attending balls. And that was not all. The duke would know I had been lying all along as well. No, I had to get us out of here before it was too late. I glanced back to where I had last seen my brother and Rose.

By Jove, they were headed this way.

Pulling Anne down with me, I crouched behind a table layered with vegetables.

"What are you doing?" the duke asked. Confusion slipping into his Irish accent.

"Just..." I patted the vegetables in front of me. "Examining the cauliflowers." Yes, because that sounded sane. I wanted to smack myself.

"Why?" the duke raised his brow, a perplexed expression on his face. At this point, the merchant leaned over the table as well.

"Ye intend to purchase that, miss?" My cheeks heated as I stared up at the merchant. I was aware of how odd I looked, crouched between the vegetables, my soft shoes squishing on the rotted cast-offs on the ground. Anne was wobbling beside me, the hem of her dress smeared with something dark that might have once been a carrot.

"Yes," I gingerly patted the cauliflower in front of me some more before handing it to the merchant. "It is a good one. Anne can attest that it is my favorite vegetable."

Anne, for what it was worth, was nodding fervently beside me. I scanned the crowd, no longer spotting John.

Perhaps he and Rose had passed us by already, but I could not be certain. I would need to be careful. I handed the merchant a bit of coin from my pocket while he handed me the cauliflower I did not want but was now saddled with. My hands were full between the bouquet of yellow flowers and the white, globed vegetable. Edmund grabbed my elbow and helped me up to standing then moved to help Anne.

Keeping an eye on the crowd, I turned to the duke and wafted my hand along my forehead in the best imitation of a woman about to faint that I could muster.

"I feel a bit tired. Perhaps we could go someplace else?"

"Are you alright? You are not overheated?" The duke immediately snatched my hand and pressed his pointer finger against my wrist, feeling for a pulse. "Nice and strong, if perhaps a tad fast," he remarked. "Mayhap a cooling beverage and a chair might help."

"Please," I said with a swift smile. The duke offered his arm again, so with a bit of juggling of the cauliflower, I took advantage of his tall frame to hide myself from view.

Using perhaps a bit too much force, I urged him down the street and away from my brother and his wife.

"There, much better," I told Edmund once we had crossed the square and reached a side street. It was not likely for my brother to find me now. I leaned against a wall while holding the cauliflower against my chest like a giant ball.

"Do you need a seat? The coffee house is not far."

I shook my head. "No, I feel much better." I thrust the cauliflower towards Edmund. "Would you like the cauliflower?"

He clutched the vegetable with an odd expression. "Thank you."

"You are welcome." I managed to flash the duke a smile.

10

Potted Eel

"A cauliflower?" Willa chortled as Anne told her what happened at our trip with the duke. She sat back in one of the tufted chairs in the sitting room, poking at a loose thread on a throw pillow.

"She patted the cauliflower as if she was patting the head of a child. You should have seen the look on the duke's face."

Peals of laughter reverberated through the room. Anne even used her little finger to wipe away wetness from beneath her eyes. I was not sure if I appreciated them laughing at my plight.

Anne joined Willa in a chair while I paced the room. "What was I supposed to do? I could not have my brother see us; besides, it isn't like there are many places to hide."

"He looked so confused." Anne brushed her hand along her face, pushing back some stray hairs, and laughed. "I cannot believe he still wanted to see you again after that whole debacle. Perhaps he *is* perfect for you."

"Very funny," I said while gritting my teeth.

"Anne might have a point," Melinda said, striding into the sitting room, a purple linen dress fluttering around her legs. "Your father asked if I would come see if you ladies would like to head outside for tea," she told Willa. "But..." she rested the tip of her finger against her chin. "While I have you here. I have been thinking that there must be a reason the bookshop sent me to this place. And just now, hearing Anne's words, I realized that perhaps it is to help Beth." Melinda pointed at me. "Perhaps the reason that I am here is to get you and the duke together."

Willa stopped picking at the pillow and stood. "Wait, that makes no sense. The duke thinks that Beth is me. Shouldn't she continue to try to get him to break things off?"

"There might be another way." Melinda glanced at me. "But first...Beth, do you like him?"

Did I like him? If I was honest with myself, I did. But how could it ever work? He thought I was a different person and we barely knew each other. What if this connection I felt was one sided?

Anne huffed; her eyes fastened on Melinda. "You do not know why you are here. It could have nothing to do with Beth." Anne looked to Willa who nodded softly with an appreciative smile. "This started as a way to help Willa. So perhaps we need to figure out how to get the duke to return to Ireland."

Willa moved to Anne's side and clasped her hand, threading their fingers. "Thank you for thinking of me." She smiled at Anne. "Though as long as the outcome is that I remain un-married, I am open for other suggestions. I may have started this whole mess but what is it that you want, Beth?" Willa asked.

I sighed, resting my head against my palms. "I do not know. Does it even matter whether or not I like him? This entire time he has been under the impression that he has been spending time with the daughter of a marquis. If he knew the real me, he might not like me. My brother might be wealthy but he does not have a title. What if marrying someone with a title is all he cares about?"

"Then it is his loss," Willa said firmly.

Melinda pursed her lips. "And what if he feels the same?"

What if he did? That was a question I might not be ready for yet. Besides, Melinda had no right to meddle in my affairs. "I think you have intervened in enough people's lives; I do not need any assistance." I walked the few steps to the settee and sank down into its plush cushions. My chest deflated.

How was I going to face the duke again? There was no good way to end this without being found out. And I doubted that he'd want to see me once he did. Despite everything I could not help but want more. His presence had turned into something I craved. His face haunted my dreams. I could still feel the touch of his hand as it trailed along my skin. Every fiber of my being wanted more.

I breathed in slowly, before looking at Melinda. "He is not going to want me once he finds out. I cannot tell him now."

Willa shrugged. "Then do not tell the duke yet. Continue courting him and wait for the right time."

I bit my lip. "When would that be?"

Anne crossed her arms. "Beth, you aren't genuinely considering continuing with this charade, are you? What about your brother and Rose? You came so close to being caught today."

"But I was not, and hopefully next time the duke will take me somewhere further away from our London rental house."

"So, you have decided?" Melinda asked.

I nodded.

Melinda grinned. "Alright, let's get to matchmaking."

* * *

After tea with the marquis, Anne and I returned home. The driver dropped us off in front of the townhouse near Covent Garden. Instead of using the front door, we walked around through the side gate. There, in the enclosed back garden, Rose and my brother were cuddled up together on a bench.

"Welcome home, we haven't seen you all day," Rose said, glancing up from a book. She closed the pages and set it aside. Next to her, John did the same with the paper he was reading. "Did you have fun with your friend, Willa?"

"Yes, we chatted and had tea with her father."

"The Marquis of Bambreich, correct?" John asked.

"He and Willa are very kind," Anne said.

I plopped down on the outdoor furniture; Anne sat down next to me. "What did you do today?"

"Rose and I took a stroll around Covent Garden—speaking of which, have you eaten?"

Both Anne and I shook our heads.

"Excellent, we ordered some potted eel and savory pies to go. How about I ask the maid to prepare us a spread outdoors instead of in the dining room? I feel a bit puckish, and it is lovely weather outside."

"You stay, John," Rose said. "I'll go and ask." She jumped to standing and kissed John on the cheek.

"So, Anne, has any bachelor caught your attention so far?" John asked.

"Not yet."

John made a sound of agreement. "You both have been preoccupied with your new friendship with the daughter of the marquis. Perhaps attending another dance is in order. I did promise your mother I would try to make this year a successful one."

Anne swallowed, a strain appearing around her eyes. "I am already grateful for everything you have done."

"Nonetheless," John continued, "Lady Sybil is hosting a dance tomorrow and Rose and I are invited. You and Beth should join; there will be plenty of eligible men in attendance. Perhaps someone there might catch your eye."

Anne nodded a bit stiffly. "Oh, yes, of course. I would love to go."

John straightened his shirt. "After the dance, if there are any interested suitors, we can host a visit here."

Anne nodded unenthusiastically.

Rose returned, followed by the kitchen maid carrying a tray laden with food. I took that opportunity to whisper to Anne.

"Do you no longer wish to find a match?"

Anne squirmed. "I...do."

"That did not sound very convincing. You also declined Willa's offer to help. What changed?"

A pair of brown eyes stared back at me in accusation. She leaned towards me, keeping her voice low. "Nothing changed."

"Not the attention of a certain someone?"

Anne huffed. "I do not know what you are talking about."

"Alright, but just so you know, I would be happy for you both."

Anne paused, seeming to fumble for her words. She quickly turned her gaze away from me. "You know why I need to find a match. My family situation has not changed."

"Perhaps John can help find a different solution."

Anne clenched her hands. "Your family has done too much already."

The maid deposited the food in the middle of the out-door table.

"Thank you," Rose told her as she left. "Now, who would like to try one of the potted eels?"

"I will take one," Anne said, her voice perking up now that she could avoid the topic we had been discussing.

Rose grabbed a napkin and a spoon and handed Anne one of the ramekins with jellied eel. A decidedly fishy scent rose up from the jiggly concoction.

The strong smell was not sitting well with me. "I will take a rain check on those and take a savory pie instead."

I bit into the flaky pastry and swallowed a bite of savory meat and swede. My eyes fell on John's discarded newspaper. I swiped my hand along my mouth, getting rid of crumbs, and looked up at my brother.

"Anything new in the paper?"

John shook his head. "More of the same; where is the Gentleman Thief? What is the most anticipated event of the season? Where can a gentleman purchase the most fashion-able items?"

"Sounds fascinating."

Rose chuckled and held out a pastry for John. "There's nothing wrong with boring. I enjoy laying down and reading a book while John reads the paper. It is fun to be away from Hawthorne for a while though. Being here feels like a vacation even if I kind of miss Mrs. Avery's cooking.

John's face softened. "You just enjoy it when you can use me as a pillow."

Rose shrugged. "That is an added bonus."

11

The foundling Hospital

Dark clouds blanketed the skies today, bathing the entire world in a diffused gray. To combat the cold wind that keened as it whipped through every crevice and piece of insulation, I wore a thicker dress with an added shawl thrown around my arms instead of my regular summer wear of thinner muslin dresses.

Despite the dreary weather, I was excited to see the duke again. Although, a small voice in the back of my head told me that I was being foolish, that the duke would never entertain me if he knew the truth. My nerves got the better of me, and I could not stop fidgeting with the courser fibers of my shawl.

Anne gently smacked my hand. "Stop teasing the tassels before you unravel the whole lot." The carriage wheels clattered beneath us as we traveled across town.

"Right." I stilled my hands and pulled the shawl tighter

around me. "Anne, do you think I am being foolish?" My voice was nearly lost in the howling wind that raced past the black carriage.

"A bit," Anne said, being one to never mince words. "However, I cannot tell you what to do. Although," Anne furrowed her brow, "I would not follow Melinda's words blindly either. Who knows what reasons she has for being here? Most of which likely have nothing to do with you. All I can ask is that you are careful. And, I suppose, that whatever you do that it is your decision."

I leaned sideways and enveloped Anne in a hug. "Thank you for being my friend."

"You are welcome," Anne spluttered out before turning her head to hide the crimson shade creeping up her face. She glanced out the window.

On my side, I could see rows upon rows of houses as we headed further into the city of London. We were nearly at the rendezvous location; the Brunswick Square Gardens.

The carriage jolted to a stop, and the driver knocked on the side of the carriage.

Edmund waited for us on the sidewalk.

"Why did you want to meet us here?" I asked, popping my head out of the opening. Edmund held out his hand and helped me down the two steps and onto the ground.

After safely helping Anne to the street, he said, "I have enjoyed getting to know you, but I feel like you do not yet know much about me. Today is all about rectifying that."

I raised my brow. "And how were you planning on doing that?"

"By showing you what I do in my spare time. Come along." His face crinkled as he smiled, brightening up the dreary day. "I hope you both are ready to work."

"Work?" Anne looked to me with questions in her eyes.

Edmund chuckled. "Yes, I volunteered us to help at the Foundling Hospital."

"I have heard of charitable events happening there, but I do not believe I ever heard of a lady or a lord volunteering their time to work." Anne righted her cap and narrowed her eyes at the duke.

Edmund nodded. "I like to be hands-on. To help where it matters. Of course, donations are helpful for organizations to help those in need, but when those events are held in lavish venues with everything the ton is accustomed to, how could one ever really empathize with those born without the advantages of wealth and titles."

"You speak as if you are not a member of the ton yourself," I remarked.

The duke let out another chuckle. "I am merely invested in providing resources for the less fortunate. It is a cause very near and dear to my heart and one I fully support when I am at my home in Ireland."

The ribbon beneath my chin loosened, and I grabbed a hold of my straw hat before it could blow away. Embarrassed, I glanced up at the duke. His dark eyes watched me as a smile tugged at his lips. I straightened the hat and retied it while continuing the conversation. "That is very admirable indeed. Is that not so, Anne?"

"Very," Anne agreed.

"Which charity do you support in Ireland?"

"My main focus goes towards providing assistance for single and widowed mothers and the upbringing of orphans."

The duke's words warmed my heart. While I did love fashion and other perhaps frivolous things that I was accustomed to, I was not unaware of the disparity between John's and my lifestyle and that of the common man. Though John was a generous landowner who ensured that his tenants lived as comfortable as possible and now with the addition of Rose's school, we also worked towards getting their children a better start in life. It was perhaps small, but change had to happen somewhere.

"What drew you to those causes?"

The corner of Edmund's mouth lifted. "I suppose you could say that it is a cause that I grew up with." His words piqued my interest, but that was all Edmund said on the matter, leaving me wondering why supporting single mothers and orphans could be important to a duke.

Edmund glanced up at the gray sky before turning to us with a mischievous smile. "We should venture inside before we are caught in a rainstorm or before we are blown away by the wind." Edmund pushed the handle and opened one of two gate doors in the large wrought iron fence that blocked in the main courtyard in front of the Foundling Hospital.

We entered the courtyard, heading for the central building which was flanked by two other large dorms. We crossed the vast space to the front door. It must have been noon already since some children were playing outside despite the weather; three boys in miniature versions of a military style uniform were tossing marbles along the pavers and another was using a spinning top while onlookers marveled at the sight. A group of girls in servants' getups were playing hoops under the watchful eye of one of the nurses.

The nurse, looking rather severe, nodded as we passed her by and entered the hospital. A young woman at the front desk jumped to standing once she spotted us, brown curls peeking out from underneath her white nurse's cap. She straightened her white apron and moved around the heavy desk to greet us.

"Welcome, Your Grace and ladies. Head nurse Margaret has informed me that you would like to assist during lunch. If you could please follow me to the kitchens?"

We followed the young nurse to the kitchens where we were handed aprons. Anne looked bemused as the duke put his on without hesitation. I swiftly followed.

"What can we do to help?" I asked the young woman.

"This is where I leave you. I have to return to the front desk," the nurse said. She pointed at another woman switching out what appeared to be large troughs of slop onto a rolling cart. "You can help nurse Hettie to dispense the food to the children."

Nurse Hettie was a woman of few words. In a brisk pace, she rolled the cart of food through the hallways, while doling out small slips of information.

"The boys are housed in the left wing while the girls are in the right."

"We are helping with feeding the boys today, then?" Anne said.

Nurse Hettie uttered a sound of agreement, while her shoes squeaked along the floor. Before we reached the dining hall, I became aware of a cacophony of noise that became ever louder as we neared the double doors. A sound that only a bunch of boys crammed together in a single room could produce; plates clanked against tables, and the high-pitched prattle of who knows how many combined voices of young boys echoed from the rafters.

"The boys receive schooling until they become of an age where they can either be apprenticed or join military service," Hettie provided.

"What about the girls?" Anne asked.

"They also receive schooling with additional attention to the female arts after which they can go into service and make a proper life for themselves. Now," Hettie scraped her throat loudly, dimming the noise the boys were making. The orphaned boys, perhaps four or five in age, pointed their attention to the nurse.

Hettie rolled the cart to the front of the dining hall and raised her voice. "If you can all create three orderly lines."

Edmund helped set out the food while Hettie handed each of us ladles.

"Make sure to give each child one large scoop of the meat." She pointed at the slop. "And give them a scoop of the vegetables and add a piece of bread." Her shrewd eyes glanced over us, deciding whether we understood what needed to happen. We must have made the right impression because with a nod of her head, she said, "Right, I shall return to the kitchen and will be back in a short while. Good luck."

I crossed eyes with Edmund and raised my brows. "Good luck," I muttered while the first children lined up with their empty plates.

Soon, the three of us were too busy scooping slop onto plates and handing out buns to think about anything else.

Edmund's face was bright as he smiled and welcomed each child that held out a plate towards him. While handing out food to the young boys myself, I could not help from glancing at the duke. He seemed lighter, more at home here than anywhere else I had seen him. Soft light from the high ceiling windows teased his dark hair, showing bursts of amber and gold threaded throughout. His arms flexed as he scooped portions of food.

"Can I have some food, miss?" I had to tear my eyes away from Edmund. I flashed a wide smile and bent towards the small boy in front of me. Green eyes peeked up at me from an unruly head of tawny hair, a metal tray clutched in his tiny hands. He smiled up at me a bit hesitantly.

"Of course." I scooped a good portion of meat, vegetables, and bread onto his tray. "Enjoy your lunch."

"Thank you, miss," the boy said as he left the line and another took his place.

By the end of lunch, my back was aching, and the front of my apron was covered in stains. Judging by a feeling of tautness on my cheek when I spoke, I even had some dried-up food on my face.

I was probably a dreadful sight, but the experience had been worth it. Feeding the children and working beside Edmund had been something entirely new for me. And seeing how sincere, caring, and hardworking he was did some strange things to my insides.

Oh, who was I kidding, Edmund was working his way underneath my skin. Though, I did my best to not dwell on the fact that I was deceiving him.

We said goodbye to the roomful of boys which was

relatively subdued as they all shoveled the food into their mouths. I wondered what happened in their brief lives to get them here. From what I remembered, the children were chosen based on a lottery system. Some of them might be orphans with no family members to turn to while others were the result of by-blows from respected gentlemen, given up by their unwed mothers to avoid ruin. My heart clenched at the thought of giving up my own child. My eyes rested on the small tawny-haired boy who was taking a large bite out of bread. I hoped he would grow up to be happy and healthy.

Edmund pushed the now empty cart in front of him and rolled it down the hallway, back to the kitchens.

"Ready?" Edmund asked once we had returned our aprons and I managed to request a wet rag to wipe my face. Hettie, the nurse, dumped the soiled aprons into a laundry bin while another handed me a wetted cloth.

"Yes," I said, wiping at my cheek. "Are we to return home?" I added the cloth to the laundry bin and swiped my palms across the front of my dress.

Edmund's eyes flashed to Anne. "I have one more thing I would like to do, if you ladies would be so kind as to indulge me. Do you think you have the time?"

"I am certain we can find the time a bit longer," I hurried to say. I shot Anne a specific look. "We do not have any other immediate plans."

Her head shook slightly, and I could tell she was stifling a laugh. Perhaps I had sounded a bit too eager. But I could not help it, I wanted to spend more time with Edmund. "I suppose we could," Anne added.

"Marvelous," Edmund said, righting himself. His teeth

flashed as he grinned at us. "I have been meaning to take a stroll along London Bridge, and I reckoned now would be lovely, to give us a chance to stretch our legs."

"During a storm?" Anne raised a brow. I kind of agreed. The straw hat that was a gift from Edmund had nearly blown away earlier. But if it was what the duke wanted then I was not going to say no.

I cleared my throat. "It might be refreshing, wouldn't you say?"

Edmund's eyes crinkled. "You read my mind. A good breeze to blow the cobwebs away."

We said goodbye to Hettie and the other nurses in the kitchens, then walked past the front desk.

"Come again," the brown-haired nurse said, standing up. "Thank you for assisting with lunch; the children appreciate it."

"I enjoyed helping out," I told her.

We crossed the threshold into the now empty courtyard.

"We should perhaps have an umbrella ready?" Anne said, glancing up at the sky. The gray clouds blanketing the heavens had darkened even more.

Now that Anne mentioned it, the outdoor smell had changed to something fresher and wilder. The scent of incoming rain tickled my nostrils. The wind had also picked up speed, lashing at my hair. I pulled my shawl around my shoulders and tied a small knot in the front so I would not lose it in a sudden gale.

Even if I did not want to, I had to admit that going for a walk did not seem like the brightest idea.

"Perhaps we should postpone our walk of the London

Bridge to another day." I did not yet want to say goodbye to the duke, but traversing the bridge while raining did not sound wise, especially with the regular heavy traffic. A carriage wheel hitting one ill placed puddle and my entire dress could be soaked.

Edmund inclined his head, his charming smile warming my heart. "The decision is yours, as always, but if you shall indulge me, I will make certain it will not be a waste of your time."

When he gazed at me with his dark eyes, how could I not agree. "Oh, alright."

We crossed the courtyard and Edmund opened the gate to let Anne and me through. He moved between us as we walked along the sidewalk. I shivered a bit, and he placed his arm around me.

"Let us procure an umbrella before we venture to the bridge."

We walked about a block until we reached a shop selling umbrellas. Edmund purchased a blue and white tipped one from the seller then we returned outdoors. He handed the umbrella to Anne who tucked the handle around the crook of her arm. Edmund held out a hand to passing traffic until a hackney cab stopped in front of us.

It was but a short ride to the London Bridge. I stepped out of the cab, nodding at the driver, followed by Anne and the duke. Anne remained behind us, swinging the umbrella in her hands as she gave us as much privacy as she could while still seeming proper. Of course, none of what we were doing could be called proper. But Anne was dead set on fulfilling her chaperon duties wherever she could so she was at the very minimum able to fulfill by my brother's wishes, if not by heart, at least in spirit.

My arm hooked around the crook of Edmund's arm. He smiled lightly, showing off his straight, white teeth.

"See here," he said, pulling me towards the weathered, low, stone wall that lined the bridge on either side. I leaned my arms on the edge and glanced in the direction that he was pointing. From a few cloud breaks, a soft yellow sunlight burst through the darkness until it lit up streaks of water on the Thames. The entire sight was ethereal.

"This is what I wanted you to see," Edmund whispered in my ear. "Most people enjoy sightseeing on a sunny day and, of course, blue skies and sun-soaked fields are pretty, but I have found that the most beautiful things reveal themselves when there is a hint of darkness."

"It is lovely." I leaned forward, peering out over the Thames.

"Yes, she is."

I turned my head and caught Edmund gazing at me, his eyes soft and warm. Blushing, I swallowed to wet my dried-up throat. The sky rumbled and small droplets landed on my arms and on his hair and eyelashes. The duke appeared as something out of a dream. Before I knew it, the sky broke completely, drenching us in cold droplets.

Anne opened the umbrella and hurried towards us. "Come shelter underneath here." The rain whipped down at us, turning our surroundings into a blur.

Edmund glanced at me, his smile devious as his curls plastered against forehead, weighed down by the rain. He held out his hand in invitation "Trust me. Let us run." My eyes widened and I managed a quick nod before he grasped my hand and I followed him, feet pounding the pavement.

"Wait, what are you doing?" Anne called after us.

I burst out laughing while my slippers squelched against the wet stone. Edmund laughed with me. My dress was soaked and my hair was drenched against the sides of my face, but I did not care. Somehow the rain had made Edmund even more attractive; his hair an even darker, glossy black and his well-cut clothing wet and sticking to his impressive body.

We continued running until Edmund veered off and pulled me into one of the empty alcoves lining the bridge.

"Do you think Anne will be awhile?" he asked, breathless.

"I would imagine so," I answered haltingly. My chest heaved as I struggled to catch my breath. It was nice to be out of the rain, sheltered beneath the small stone alcove. With the heavy lashings turning the outside into a blur, it felt as if the duke and I were in a different world.

Edmund closed the space between us, his eyes sweeping my body. "I hope you will forgive my imprudence, but I would very much like to kiss you."

My heart thudded loudly in my chest. Water puddled at my feet.

"May I?"

"Yes," I breathed only a second before he grasped my face and claimed my lips. We were both chilled, but soon a new kind of heat moved through me, warming me from my core. Our lips danced, and after opening my mouth, his tongue darted in and twirled with mine. His hand cupped the back of my neck and pulled me in tighter. I rocked against his body, swept up in his motions. Kissing the duke felt like it was meant to be. His touch set my skin aflame. Edmund's nose brushed mine when he deepened his kiss, and everything around me faded away.

There was only him and me.

Slowly, he untangled his lips from mine so he could look at me. "You are the most beautiful woman I have ever seen." His eyes darted to my reddened lips, a smile tugging at his lips. "Thank you for letting me show you the London Bridge today."

"I am glad you did," I added a bit bashful.

Wet footsteps headed our way. Most likely, Anne catching up with us again. The duke stepped back to a more proper distance before she saw us.

"There you are," Anne said, ducking into the alcove. "Why all the running?" Her eyes flashed to my face, and she gave me a knowing glance. "I see..."

Despite his drowned appearance, Edmund pretended he had no idea what Anne inferred.

Anne crossed her arms. "Perhaps we should call it a day? My friend needs a wardrobe change after all."

"Umm, yes. Perhaps we should," I said with a shy glance at Edmund. I crossed my arms to cover the rather translucent nature of my now wet dress.

Anne pulled up the umbrella, shielding us from the rain, and walked us back down the bridge.

Once we reached a cab, Edmund bowed. "Until next time."

12

Game Of Whist

"What happened to the both of you?" John let out a boisterous laugh at the sight of Anne and myself. "Fallen into the Thames?"

Bartley held open the front door while Anne and I stood in the foyer, water dripping down the hems of our dresses, adding to a growing puddle beneath our feet. Anne set the blue umbrella down against the wall.

"I think you both shall be glad to hear that the dance at Lady Sybil's manor has been canceled due to the weather." John quirked his brow, his cheeks dimpling. He held out his hand for my soaked straw hat while the butler closed the door behind us.

It was a good thing John reminded me; I had completely forgotten about the dance and did not mourn its cancellation. I shivered in my drenched dress, teeth clacking together. Anne looked a bit more composed than me but only slightly.

"Bartley, perhaps you can arrange for two tubs to be filled and brought to their rooms? I am certain Anne and Beth would like to clean themselves and warm up."

"Right away, sir." The butler nodded and headed to the servants' quarters.

John dropped my dripping hat on top of the entryway bench then held out his hands again. "Here, let me take both your shawls and go ahead upstairs. I will make sure there are some hot beverages waiting when you return to the sitting room."

I deposited the wet fabric in his hands and grabbed the sides of my dress. Lifting the hem, I climbed the stairs to my bedroom. Anne followed suit.

I laughed and turned towards Anne when we reached the second-floor landing. "You were the one carrying an umbrella, but yet you are just as waterlogged as I am when I was the one running through the rain."

Anne sneezed and brushed back some of her brown hair. "No need to remind me." She rolled her eyes at me. "We should have left for home after the Foundling Hospital."

I dropped the hem of my dress. "I am glad we went. It was enlightening to see Edmund interacting with the children, endearing."

"And I am certain you enjoyed what happened after you both ran from me as well." Anne's brow lifted, a teasing smirk on her face.

"Of course, did I not tell you our first evening here that I wanted to dance and flirt with a gentleman, and that I might even let him kiss me?" I was joking of course, but the memory of kissing Edmund in the rain sent shivers up and down my spine.

Anne sniffled again and sneezed.

I was cold, and Anne's lips had turned pale; we had plenty of time to chat after we warmed up. "We should get out of these wet clothes and get ready for a bath."

Anne nodded and turned into her room.

Footsteps marched up the stairs, and two servants carried up the tubs. One entered Anne's room with a swift knock, while the other nodded as he passed me and deposited the second tub in my room. Next followed maids carrying buckets of steaming water. I followed them into my own room. The scullery maid emptied the bucket into the tub then moved to the fireplace to poke up the fire. Embers sparked and flames shot up from the coal that had almost been consumed into ash. She added another few pieces of coal, filling my room with a pleasant warmth.

She returned the poke to its stand and swiped her hands on her apron before standing. "I'll be right back with more water, miss."

"Thank you," I told the maid.

It took a few more trips with the bucket to get the tub filled to a sufficient level. I managed to take my wet dress off despite it sticking to my bare skin then fumbled with the hooks on the back of my stays and rolling down the stockings. I dropped the sodden clothes to the floor with a wet squelch and stepped into the tub, letting myself slide down into the heated water. The maid picked up my clothes and took them with her on her way downstairs.

I sighed deeply as the heat worked to soothe my muscles and drive away the cold that had settled within my bones. Sliding down even further, I managed to dunk my head, ridding myself of the scent of earthy rainwater that clung to my hair. When I returned to a seated position, I grabbed a bar of lavender soap from beside the tub and lathered up my hands. I lifted my palms up to my face and inhaled deeply, eyes shut as the tension exited my body.

Outside, the wind lashed against my window and howled through the smallest crevices in the wood, but inside, I was warm and comfortable, soaking in the water. I was glad I did not need to dress up and attend a ball this evening. Between helping at the Foundling Hospital and kissing Edmund on top of the London Bridge, I had my fair share of excitement today. I rubbed the bar of soap along my skin. This had been the second time the duke and I had kissed. I bit my lip and shook my head, lathering up my shoulders and chest. That he had initiated it the second time could only mean that he was interested, right? It meant he liked me for who I was and not just for being the supposed daughter of a marquis?

This whole situation gnawed at me. I needed to tell the duke the truth about who I was and hope for the best. But how was I supposed to bring it up without scaring him off. What if he did not want to see me again after I told him the truth. The thought of never seeing Edmund again sent a pang of pain through my heart. No, I could not rush into it. I would need to be careful, delicate on how I broached the subject.

I stirred the warm water, cupping my hand to bring it up to my neck and let it rinse the soap off my skin. Stretching my limbs, I leaned my head back against the edge of the tub and remained there until the water turned tepid.

Finally, I stood and wound a towel around my body. I sat down at the vanity and wound my hair into a loose braid, tying it off with a thin yellow ribbon. This was something I could do without Estelle's help. Then, I pulled on a new chemise and a comfortable brown day dress without adding on stays.

Fully clothed, I left my room behind and ventured downstairs to the sitting room.

John was playing cards with Rose and Anne, a fire roaring behind them.

Something sweet and fragrant perfumed the air.

Anne took a sip from a porcelain cup and returned it the low decorative table in front of them, her upper lip tinted brown. She looked up at me from behind the cards she was holding in her left hand and licked her lips. "Welcome back. We almost thought you had fallen asleep in there."

Rose patted the seat beside her. "Come sit down and join us. Would you like some chocolate? There is more." Anne was wearing a simple day dress while Rose had opted for her trousers and one of John's shirts. John had no need to object to her unconventional dress if they did not leave the house. While I sat down next to Rose, my brother grabbed another cup and poured thick, silky chocolate from a pot and handed it to me.

Rose lowered her cards onto the table. "We can reshuffle and start a new game. With the four of us we could play a game of whist?"

I sipped from my chocolate and nodded. "I would like that."

John gathered the cards and reshuffled the deck. "Rose and I against the two of you, then?" He raised his brow at Anne and me.

I scooted back in my seat and leaned back. "You are on. What is the wager?"

John narrowed his eyes and glanced to his wife as he considered. "What do you think?"

Rose puckered her lips and tapped her finger against her upper lip. "In the spirit of fun, how about the losing team play the victors a song?"

"Those are not very high stakes, but I suppose I shall accept." I grinned and took another sip of chocolate, the rich drink coating my mouth.

Anne laughed. "Will you take requests?"

"I doubt that will be necessary." John sounded amused as he moved clockwise, slapping down cards in front of us until only one card remained in his hand. "Three of clubs." He laid the trump card in the middle of the table. "Since you are on my left, how about you start the game," he told Rose.

I fixed my braid behind my back and picked up my down-facing cards. Rose added a king of clubs to the table, but I did not have any clubs in my possession, so I laid down the lowest value card I had which was a two of hearts. Anne went next with a seven of clubs.

John smirked and laid down a jack of clubs. "Looks like this trick is ours." He grabbed the cards and stacked them by Rose's side.

An hour or so later we had reached the final round. Both

John and Rose and Anne and I had an even number of points. It was Anne's turn to lay down the trump card.

"Three of hearts," she said, depositing it on the table. I scooted forward, checking the remainder of my cards. She raised her brows at me, a hint of a smile. I grinned. No one had deposited any high value cards for hearts, yet.

"I think this will be our game," John said, adding the queen of hearts. Rose followed with a nine.

My grin grew wider. I slapped down my king. "And this trick is ours. Now let's hear it for our victory."

I gathered the cards and showed our collection of won cards.

John hung his head. "I cannot believe I have been beaten by my younger sister." He glanced at me with a devious glint. "Can I interest you in a rematch?"

I shook my head firmly then smirked. "No, Anne and I would like to enjoy our winnings now."

John exaggerated a sigh and slapped his leg before standing. "Oh well, it was worth a try." He held out his hand for Rose. "How about you play the piano and I sing?"

Rose grabbed John's hand and moved towards the piano forte. Glancing back, she laughed and said, "Congratulations." She sat down on the bench and flipped through the sheet music. "Will this one work?" She pointed at a song. John leaned forward and nodded.

"Alright, I hope you enjoy the song." John straightened, sticking out his chest. Rose played a popular folk song while John sung. My brother was a serviceable singer; he managed the notes and sounded pleasant enough, but was not impressive like William. However, hearing him sing as our winnings made listening ten times more enjoyable.

I grinned widely when John finished his last note and clapped. He pulled Rose up to standing, and together they bowed.

He straightened and smiled, holding Rose's hand. "Who is next?"

13

⸎

Millefruit Biscuits

"You will have to come to the Farnsby's ball with me," Willa said when she found Anne and myself enjoying tea in the back garden.

Our butler inclined his head after showing Willa to us. "I will leave you to it, Ms. Easton and Ms. Blakeley."

"Thank you, Bartley. Perhaps you could ask Mary to bring out another cup and more tea?"

"Right away, miss."

A little disheveled in appearance, Willa slumped down into one of the outdoor chairs.

I leaned forward, setting down my empty cup. "Now what were you saying about a ball?"

"The duke sent a letter to my father asking if I would join him at the Farnsby's ball. I was not able to lift it from the stack of correspondence before my father had already opened it." A small pucker formed between Willa's brows.

"When is it?" Anne asked.

"This evening. I will have to return home soon because my father is excited that I received an invitation and wants to see me dressed properly." Willa's eyes flitted to me. "You can come, can't you? The duke will be expecting to see you there."

"Yes, of course." I did not have any other obligations plus I would never give up a chance to see the duke.

Willa relaxed and turned her gaze to Anne. "You are coming as well, I hope? I need someone to keep me company while Beth is off flirting with the duke."

Anne nodded, her lip twitching into a smile. "I will be there."

"Good. The ball starts at eight."

Mary returned carrying a tray; she deposited a cup in front of Willa and added a plate with Prince of Wales biscuits and millefruit biscuits along with a fresh pot of tea on the table.

"Thank you, Mary," I said, taking the pot of tea and pouring Willa a cup. After topping up Anne and my own cups, I grabbed the hard Prince of Wales biscuit and dunked it in my tea.

Willa nibbled on a millefruit biscuit. "Are these not supposed to be for dessert to be dunked in sweet wine?"

"Yes, but Rose likes to eat biscuits with tea so we have started eating them like this instead."

Willa grinned and dunked the last piece in her tea. "I might have to ask my cook to do the same during tea time; I am certain my father would like having a biscuit with tea. Perhaps we could add those rolled wafers."

Seeing Willa brought something else to my mind. It had

been a few days since I had seen the bookshop owner. "Is Melinda still visiting your home?"

Willa shrugged and set down her cup of tea. "My papa and Melinda have been spending a lot of time together....Having her around has been helpful with distracting Papa from what we have been doing. If Melinda was not spending this much time with him, I am afraid he would have been more insistent on meeting the duke himself, and that would certainly ruin our deception."

"Good thing she showed up when she did then."

* * *

I would see the duke again at the Farnsby's ball. I sighed in front of my wardrobe. This would be our first time at a ball together after our initial meeting; I wanted to look my best.

"Blue always suits you," Anne offered from her position at the end of my bed.

I thumbed through the dresses; some were thicker woven fabrics while others were silky and smooth as the fabric slipped through my fingers. My hand stopped at a navy-blue gown. I pulled the dress out of the wardrobe and held it in front of me, swishing the skirt.

I beamed up at Anne. "This one?"

Anne nodded and stretched her legs, planting her stockinged feet onto the floor. She stood and moved to a sideboard, rifling through the container of accessories until she picked up a silver ribbon.

"With this underneath your bust. And..." She glanced over the accessories once more to pick up earrings, a necklace, and some hair adornments. "These." She smirked and wiggled her brow. "You will look irresistible. The duke will be entranced."

I snorted, scratching the back of my neck. "I hope so." I draped the gown over a chair. "I just wonder how I should broach the subject of—"

"Your switched identity."

"Yes. What if I can find a good time to tell him this evening? Or perhaps I should prove our compatibility during the ball and confront him another day. What do you think?"

Anne hummed to herself. "It might be better to wait until the two of you are alone. We do not know how the duke will take being deceived."

"You are right." I moved to the bowl on top of my vanity and filled it with some fresh water from a pitcher. I splashed some on my face then dabbed my skin dry with a cloth.

"Would you like some rouge?" I grabbed a small metal tin from my vanity and held it out to Anne. She dipped her finger and swiped some onto her cheeks, rubbing it in until a natural, soft, rosy glow was achieved. I dabbed some of the rose oil mixed with carmine onto my own cheeks and lips.

Estelle entered my room. "Ready for your hair, mademoiselle?"

My French ladies' maid took a stand behind me while I planted myself on the vanity stool. She deftly coiled my hair up from the nape of my neck, armed with pins. Anne handed Estelle silver strands to weave into my hair.

The finished result made me seem celestial, shimmering silver peeking through my hair. Anne returned to my side with the earrings and necklace. She fastened the necklace while I threaded the earrings through my ears; drops of gems encased in silver trailed down my collarbone while a similar design dangled to the base of my neck.

I gaped at my own reflection. I looked beautiful, and I was certain Edmund would think the same.

Switching places with Anne, I continued getting dressed. Estelle worked Anne's hair into an equally beautiful style. I could not stop smiling; I was looking forward to seeing Edmund.

14

The Farnsby's Ball

"Will you dance with me?" Edmund held out his hand in invitation. I slid my gloved hand into his and let him take me to the dance floor. Anne and Willa flashed me encouraging smiles from the corner where they were standing.

The Farnsby's ball was packed with people dancing and chatting, staff circling the room with refreshments, and artists striking poses in more revealing outfits than the guests dared. Though, I spotted a few young women wearing pink stockings beneath their cream and white colored dresses.

The duke pulled me into his arms as the first notes of a waltz started playing. Closing my eyes briefly, I inhaled his fresh scent, a cologne which mixed wonderfully with his own natural odor.

"I have missed you," Edmund whispered as he placed his hand on my waist. His fingers pressed into my flesh. I followed his lead with the footwork, drawing triangles along the floor.

All around us couples were doing the same, forming a beautiful mosaic of dancers.

"We have barely been parted." I gazed up at him, once again noticing how expressive his dark eyes were as they bored into mine. Edmund seemed to have been born with a sensual and teasing smile on his face.

"A single moment away from you feels like an eternity."

Had the duke truly said that? Despite making my heart flutter, I covered my mouth and smothered a giggle.

Edmund's eyes crinkled into a bashful smile. "Too trite?"

I could not help snorting. "A bit."

"I suppose, I cannot help it. Whenever I am around you all I want to do is spout off flowery words." Edmund twirled me around. "Perhaps my words would be perceived better if I recited works by Byron? My own are not up to the task I am afraid."

"Well, when you put it like that...I do not mind it at all." I sighed contentedly. "Spending time with you has been wonderful." Edmund and I swayed to the music, focused solely on each other.

"I concur, I never tire of seeing you." Edmund's thumb caressed the spot on my waist. He quieted for a moment as we continued our turns about the dance floor. His face took on a pinched look, eyes darkening with whatever was crossing his mind.

I missed a step as I caught his expression. "Edmund, what is wrong?"

My voice pulled him out of his reverie, and the frown on his face dissipated. "Nothing, my lovely Willa. Nothing at all."

Willa...the name stung every time the duke used it. It was a stark reminder that I was still deceiving Edmund. I needed to come clean and clear my conscience, come what may. He deserved the truth. And I hoped that his feelings for me would be strong enough to overcome my lies and deceit. Perhaps tomorrow I could take us somewhere private...

Edmund leaned forward, his lips brushing my ear. "Perhaps we can find a place to speak later this evening? I have some things I would like to say to you." There was a certain skittish quality to his gaze, his eyes darting away from mine.

I looked at him once he straightened. "Yes."

He nodded. "The end of the season is mere weeks away. I cannot wait any longer."

Wait for what? I wanted to ask him, but the song ended, and the duke let go of my waist.

"I shall find you," he muttered, then bowed deeply before leaving me behind on the dance floor.

With a last glance at the duke, I returned to my friends. Willa was busy fitting an entire cracker with caviar into her mouth while Anne stared at her, bright-eyed and bemused.

"Beth, good effort keeping your hands away from each other," Willa said after chewing and swallowing the bite of food. Anne snatched another hors d'oeuvre from a circulating waiter and handed it to Willa.

Willa flashed Anne a wide smile. "Thank you."

"Willa has a point," Anne said after returning Willa's smile. "He looked as if he was going to kiss you right then and there. The scandal if that would have happened."

My eyes widened in shock. "Anne, you do not need to announce it to the entire room. Lower your voice."

Willa snorted chewing the other hors d'oeuvre.

Anne motioned at the room full of the Farnsby's guests. "Everyone is too occupied with dancing and drinking to pay attention to us wallflowers."

"Still..." I leaned in closer to them. "Edmund did ask to speak to me later this evening. He said he would come and find me. I wonder what it is he wants to tell me."

Anne shot me an exasperated look. "You cannot tell me you have no idea what he wants to tell you."

I shook my head, worried now. "It cannot be, not yet. I have not told him the truth."

"Yes, but he does not know that." Willa shrugged empathetically. "He is under the impression that you are me and that my father is not only encouraging the match but indeed actively sought it out."

"And he clearly likes you," Anne added.

"Fair point." I fidgeted with the ribbon around my waist and frowned. "What am I supposed to do? I cannot let him propose without knowing the truth."

Anne nodded, pursing her lips. "When he takes you somewhere private, you should ask to speak first. Tell him the truth. It will be up to the duke whether he accepts your apology, but at least he will know the truth and so will you. If he truly loves you, he will make the right decision, and if he does not then you will be better off without him."

Anne squeezed my hand. "I think you need something to fortify yourself with." She glanced around until she spotted a server carrying drinks. I stayed with Willa until Anne returned with three glasses of punch.

Sweet, fruit-flavored alcohol slid down my throat as I tipped back some of the punch. The drink was heavily fortified with rum. I needed to be careful with the amount I imbibed; I wanted to calm my nerves, not get myself drunk.

Willa swallowed some of her drink and hissed. "That is one of the strongest glasses of punch I have encountered. By my count, half of those attending shall be deep within their cups and snoring in their chairs before long."

"Perhaps we could take some air to clear my head?"

Willa and Anne joined me as we wound our way past dancing guests and dandies drinking, the ballroom filled with raucous laughter and merriment.

We stepped outdoors; the back garden was lit up with burning torches to chase away the dark. The refreshing evening breeze did wonders for my constitution. Nerves made me run hot and sweaty. I patted the sides of my face with a handkerchief and joined Willa and Anne on a bench.

"Where is Melinda?" I asked Willa. "I have not seen her in a while."

Willa snorted. "She has taken a liking to my father and is occupying a lot of his time."

"That is a good thing...right?"

"It is." Willa rolled her eyes and sniffed. "I like Melinda; she is a bit of an odd duck, but she is kind. And having her around to distract my father is also beneficial. Without her, our scheme more than likely would have been found out already. My father is not stupid." Willa paused and looked at Anne. "I have also enjoyed spending time with you."

Anne coughed and glanced in another direction. I sensed something brewing between my two friends.

"However, it is strange to see my father hanging onto every word of another woman. He has been so different. I cannot recall the last time I have seen him smile like this. It worries me as well since Melinda is..." Willa lowered her voice despite no one else being around, "a time-traveler."

Anne and I nodded.

"I am worried that he will be hurt when she eventually leaves," Willa continued.

"Has Melinda said she was leaving?"

"Not yet." Willa crossed her legs.

"Then perhaps you could ask her when you see her next. It might alleviate your worries."

"I suppose."

"Would you like me to be there when you do?" Anne asked Willa.

Willa smiled at Anne, her cat-like eyes softening. "I would." She sighed and smacked her thigh. "Alright, let us take a turn about the garden. It is getting a bit cold sitting still."

"Would you rather return indoors?" Anne took off her shawl and handed it to Willa.

"Not yet," Willa said, draping the fabric around her shoulders. Soft chords floated out over the patio, and she turned to face Anne. Willa reached for Anne's hand, grasping it gently. Away from staring eyes, their movements started to mirror the ones Edmund and I had made on the dance floor earlier. I backed away, sensing they could use a private moment together.

"I will be back later," I murmured before returning to the ballroom.

Inside, I did a turn about the room by myself and picked up a different hors d'oeuvre with another glass of punch which I sipped delicately this time. A gentleman asked for a dance, but I politely declined.

"There you are," Edmund's voice said behind me. I twirled around to face him. "Do you have time to talk?"

My feelings were mixed; I was glad to be near Edmund again, but then I was also dreading what would be coming next. I set my half eaten hors d'oeuvre and glass of punch on a side table and swallowed. "I do. Anne and…Beth are occupied elsewhere." My skin tingled, and my stomach felt a bit drawn. It was now or never. I just hoped the alcohol helped to keep my composure.

"Follow me," Edmund said. "If we cross the room and leave in turns, I doubt anyone will notice us missing. We will need some more privacy than can be given anywhere at Farnsby's Manor. For what I would like to discuss, we do not need to be overheard."

My stomach fluttered. "Alright…"

"Dear, Willa. Let us get to the foyer. I will leave the manor first and wait for you with a carriage at the end of the path. You can follow me fifteen minutes later and none shall be the wiser."

"Now?"

"Now," he nodded. He strode around the dance floor heading towards the exit, anticipation or excitement evident in his decisive long strides. He wasted no more time. I followed, keeping up pace behind him.

"Beth Easton," a girl bellowed.

I cringed at the sound of my name and turned my head to the offending voice. No, no, no, no, no. It was Arabella. I needed to leave, pretend I had not heard her. I turned my head away and continued walking, hoping the girl would give up.

"Beth, it is you." She caught up with me and grabbed my hand.

Edmund noticed the commotion and stopped. He glanced back at the girl and me.

"It has been a while since the luncheon at Hyde Park," Arabella said, oblivious to my distress. She chatted happily as if we were the best of friends. I wanted to disappear into the ground and never return.

"I need to go," I hurried out, hoping Arabella would stop speaking so I could make my escape without causing a scene; however, Edmund returned to my side.

His expression darkened as he tried to figure out what was happening. "You must be mistaken; this is Willa Balfour," Edmund told Arabella. My face turned an ugly shade of red.

Arabella gave Edmund a short, confused glance. "No, this is Beth Easton from Westbridge. Our families are acquainted with one another."

Edmund turned deathly silent, his brows furrowing and eyes darkening as he glanced down at me. "Is what this girl is saying true? Your name is not Willa...?" His cold voice chilled my heart.

"I-Edmund-I..." I choked on my own words.

Arabella stood gaping, confused at our interaction. "What is going on?"

"I need to leave." Edmund swept out of the room without another word. My heart sank, leaving me feeling hollow.

"What was that?" Arabella asked. She was glancing around the room with an expression of shock, but I had no time for her.

"Arabella, not now," I told the girl before grabbing my skirts and hurrying after the duke. I did not care about what people might think of me. Arabella had ruined everything. I had been so close to telling Edmund the truth. Mere minutes away from leaving the ball with him. And now...my chances were ruined. Utterly hopeless.

I ran as fast as I was able on the slippery floor. The door-man's eyes widened as he saw me racing for the entrance. He swiftly opened the door, and I continued running.

"Edmund, wait!" I shouted at the figure of the duke walk-ing down the path to the front gate.

His shoulders stiffened at the sound of my voice, but he continued his pace.

"Edmund, please. Let me explain."

Finally, he stopped. "I think I have heard enough."

"I never meant to lie. It started...My friend Willa asked me to switch places."

"Oh, so there is a Willa?"

I winced at the tone of his voice. "Yes, I was doing her a favor. She never wanted to get married or be courted by a man. I never expected to meet someone like you, and I also never expected to like you. But here I am."

"Here you are," he said, his face drawn and sallow. "Why not confess sooner? Why did I have to hear it from some-one else?"

"I was going to." I waved my arms. "I planned to tell you once we were somewhere private."

"You had plenty of chances before tonight."

"I..." I sighed. "You are right. I should have. I liked you, and I was worried you would turn away from me once you found out I was not the daughter of a marquis."

Edmund's face turned to steel, his eyes avoiding my gaze. For a moment, he stood there on the gravel, something warring on his face, before he finally spoke. His musical accent had gone flat and cold. "You were correct. I have had enough. This is where we break our acquaintance."

Edmund swallowed, Adam's apple bobbing, and stuck his hands in his pockets. He was every part the uninterested gentleman; I wondered how much of it was true. "I shall leave and if we ever meet again, I shall do my best to pretend we are strangers."

Edmund refused to look at me; his gaze passed me by, focusing instead on something to the side, as if I was beneath his notice.

My heart broke into thousands of sharp shards, slicing my insides. My face crumbled. "Edmund..." My voice hitched as I reached out my hand towards him.

He withdrew his arm from my reach and stepped back, his gaze never once touching me. "Good day to you, Ms. Easton."

15

A Large, Too Hot, Swallow Of Tea

The ride back to the house had passed in a blur. I went upstairs without speaking to anyone, merely climbed the stairs and let myself fall down on my bed.

My chest squeezed so tightly I could scarcely draw breath. Was this what it felt like to have your heart broken? How foolish had I been to fall in love with a man that was never meant to be mine. A sob slipped out while my hot tears soaked the bedspread beneath me. I curled up into a ball on top of my small bed.

The duke had looked so cold; just remembering his face made my heart clench. Now that he knew the truth, it made sense that he did not want me. What did I have to offer him? Why was I so naive?

My nose was stuffed up and my eyes hurt. Perhaps John

had been right all along; perhaps I should have stayed in Westbridge.

The door to my room creaked open then my body jostled as Anne plopped down beside me. She gently laid her hand on my back. I rubbed my tear-stained eyes with the back of my hand, turning my head up towards her.

"You can say it..." Anne was quiet, but I could guess what my friend had been thinking. I had brought all of this on myself.

"Say what?" She brushed a few sticky clumps of hair back from my face and tucked them behind my ear.

I let out a rattling sigh. "You can tell me that you have said this would happen. That you were right from the start and I should have listened to you. I don't know what I was thinking agreeing to Willa's scheme. Perhaps if I had listened to you, I would not be in this predicament."

"Beth—" Anne stopped, her expression sad. Usually, she could sound a bit bossy, but now her voice was soft, hesitant. "I have never wanted you to be anything other than happy. It pains me to see you laying here in tears." She squeezed my shoulder as I propped myself up. "You are my most treasured friend. I can be a bit harsh in my warnings, but that is merely because I care, and I do not want to see you get hurt. I am sorry that this scheme between you and the duke turned out the way that it did. It is plain to see that you harbor strong feelings for him."

I closed my eyes. "I think I may love him."

Anne nodded as she processed my words. "The duke most likely will not want to speak to you again."

My heart clenched at the thought of never seeing the duke

again, to never again feel his hand slip around mine as he led me to the dance floor. A fresh wave of tears slid down my cheeks. I had to look like a mess with my hair in disarray, red eyes, runny nose, and tears streaking down my face.

"I know."

I propped myself up more, sweeping my feet beneath me.

Anne slung her arms around me, pulling me into the warmth of her embrace. "I am here, whenever you need to talk." She squeezed me a bit tighter to emphasize her words. Then she pulled back, her tone once again firm. "We should get you some tea. Everything seems better once you have had some tea."

Anne nodded briskly and strode out of the room, presumably to order a maid to bring some freshly brewed tea to my room. A couple of minutes later, Anne returned. She snatched the cloth hanging from the edge of my washing basin and dipped a point into the water, wetting it. Then she returned to my side.

"How about we clean you up," she said, swiping the salt tracks from my cheeks with the wetted side of the cloth. Then she found a brush and combed out the angry snarls of hair jutting out from my face. Once she was done, Anne took a step back to admire her work. "Much better." She set aside the brush and smiled at me. I knew what Anne was doing; Anne disliked feeling like she could not be of use so she would turn to doing tasks to help make someone feel better.

The maid dropped off a tray holding a steaming pot of tea, two cups and saucers, and a plate with a small variety of biscuits. Anne handed me an oatmeal biscuit which I greedily scarfed down, washing the crumbs away with a large, too hot, swallow of tea. My throat tightened on the food and drink, but once the uncomfortable sensation passed, the heat spread through my stomach, warming me up. Anne was right; tea did make everything seem better, even if it was only temporary. Anne gave me another biscuit before starting on her own tea.

"This might not be what you imagined," she said carefully, in between dainty sips from her cup. "However, before this, you were looking forward to attending your first London season." I opened my mouth to reply, but Anne shushed me. "Beth, there are still plenty of events to attend. Perhaps another gentleman might catch your eye. After all, there have been men visiting this house looking to be your suitor."

I swallowed my tea thickly. "I suppose." The lie tasted sour as it slipped past my lips. The duke would be more difficult to forget than that.

* * *

I spent the next few days sulking around the townhouse, only putting on a happy face whenever my brother was around. After everything that happened with Mr. Danby, I did not need John worrying about me; he might never let me leave Hawthorne again. Though Rose must have suspected something was wrong as she stopped me one morning after breakfast and pulled me aside.

"Did something happen?" she asked, her intelligent eyes locking onto mine.

I did not want to have a conversation about the whole fiasco with the duke. If I shared it with Rose, she might feel obligated to discuss it with my brother, and I did not want that to happen, nor did I want to put her in a position where she would have to lie.

"Nothing is the matter," I told Rose. "I suppose I am a bit overwhelmed from all the events.

Rose squinted her eyes, taking in my words. "You have been going to a lot of parties and those dresses and shoes are not the most comfortable." She laughed, scratching the back of her neck. "I should know, I much prefer wearing trousers and a shirt. How about you take some time to kick-back and relax; you don't need to go to parties every day."

"Relax," I murmured, nodding. I had gotten used to Rose's interesting colloquialisms. John and I had even started using some ourselves.

Rose fanned herself. "Maybe John can take us out to a park soon, let us soak up the sun. I miss the heat from back home; I need a bit more than fifteen minutes of sunshine every second Thursday of who-knows-when."

I snorted despite myself. Rose had made it known she disliked the often gray and dreary weather in England. "A day at a park would be lovely," I agreed.

"Alright," she said, smiling as she walked off. "I'll inform John of our idea."

While Rose headed towards the sitting room where John by now would be reading the newspaper, I trailed my way to the back of the house, passing Estelle near the stables as I bee-lined for the small outdoor seating area.

I had noticed Estelle frequenting the stables often, taking every chance to linger near the wooden structure, especially when a certain coachman was tending to the horses or oiling the wheels on the carriage.

Usually, I thought her infatuation with the man was adorable and I would tease her as she pinned my hair up into one of her preferred hairstyles, trying to get her to tell me about her their blossoming relationship despite her protestations. But today…I swallowed thickly, cursing the painful squeezing in my chest. No, today, seeing their shy exchanges and smiles was not giving me any joy. Today, it reminded me of my lack of romance; it reminded me of Edmund.

Biting my lip, I considered Anne's words. Perhaps I should push the duke out of my mind and throw myself back into the fray, mingle with other eligible bachelors. There was no reason to sulk; I was Beth Easton after all. I was a handsome woman with a large dowry, even if my tryst with the Edmund had made me doubt my worth. If I so chose, I could have my pick of eligible men…*but not the duke*, my mind finished. No, I could not think that way.

I stood with a huff and headed towards the stables. Estelle was leaning against the whitewashed entrance post, watching the coachman as he brushed one of the horses; a hackney pony that nibbled on the edge of his coat.

"Ms. Easton," Estelle said, dipping her head and curtsying as soon as she caught sight of me.

"Good day, Estelle, Mr. Ward," I said, nodding to the coachman before turning back to my maid. "Estelle, I have decided to open the drawing room to suitor's tomorrow, if you can make the arrangements on this short of a notice."

"Certainly, I shall inform the cook that we shall need

additional biscuits and other savories prepared right away, mademoiselle." Her eyes darted to the coachman who continued to diligently brush the pony, his arm muscles flexing beneath his shirt with every sweep of the comb. "Perhaps Mr. Ward could take me to the shops after I notify the cook and confirm the ingredients we are missing?" My maid's cheeks turned red as she finished her sentence.

The coachman glanced up at Estelle, a hint of a smile teasing at the edge of his lips.

I nodded. "Thank you, Estelle, that is an excellent idea." I turned to the coachman who laid down the comb and patted the Hackney Pony on his wide behind. "Do you have time to take Estelle into town, Mr. Ward?"

"You can call me Tom, Ms. Easton," the coachman said with a slight bow.

"Tom," I corrected with a smile.

The coachman straightened and scratched behind the pony's ear. "Since it's a quick trip, I'll harness Bonnie here. She could use the exercise." The pony bristled as if it could understand the coachman's words and felt offended.

16

Old Bond Street

Anne and Rose joined me in the drawing room as I waited for the first suitors to arrive during the morning. A few maids had prepared the table with a spread of light foods, crackers, tarts, and a large pitcher of lemonade. Earlier, Estelle had wound my hair into a circular pattern at the crown of my head with blonde whisks pulled out and curled to frame my face. I had picked my outfit; a pale pink dress with white embroidered flowers on the hemline and shoulder with elbow-length yellow gloves. For the finishing touch, I had added my late mother's pearl necklace.

Now, sitting on the love seat I shared with Anne, I knew I would make a good impression to any gentleman who came knocking.

Rose entered, inspecting the refreshments and snagging a tart, before coming to my side.

"Are you sure you want to do this?" She looked concerned.

"I don't know what is going on with you, but you don't look like you are excited about having suitors over."

My lip trembled, but I forced it to stiffen. Edmund had broken my heart and now there was only one thing left to do; get back to my own life and forget all about him.

I raised my chin. "Thank you, Rose, but I am alright. Perhaps a bit nervous but that shall pass soon enough."

Rose still seemed skeptical. "Okay then. I'll let Bartley know that you are ready."

"Thank you."

Anne turned to me. "I believe I understand why you have not told Rose anything, but she is your friend as well as your sister-in-law. Does she not deserve to know?"

"I do not know how to bring it up to Rose, and she would be obligated to tell my brother. I could not bear him finding out. You do not need to worry about me. It is over between me and the duke, and I am making sure that my feelings shall be well and buried in the past."

Anne made a scoffing sound. "Just think things through first."

"Mr. Eddington," Bartley said in his deep voice as he showed in the first gentleman. The butler was a comforting presence in our London rental.

Mr. Eddington plastered his legs together and ceremoniously bowed at us, one hand held elegantly behind his back. "Ms. Easton and Ms. Blakeley, thank you for inviting me into your home this fine day."

"The pleasure is all mine," I said. "Please, have a seat and feel free to take some refreshments." I was glad that the man returned to standing because his heavily starched cravat appeared to be cutting off his oxygen.

"Mary is on her way with tea," Bartley said with a sincere nod before stalking out of the room.

"So, Mr. Eddington, what do you do?"

"I am an avid horseman. Such an invigorating sport, do you not agree?"

I forced myself to smile. "I do enjoy riding. When home at Hawthorne, I often take a ride around the estate."

Mary passed around the tea and left while Bartley introduced more gentlemen. An hour later, Anne and I were both doing our best to pay attention to Mr. Eddington, Mr. Garrett, and Mr. Lovett, but both our attention spans had been stretched to their maximum capacities.

It was not that the men were unpleasant or not handsome; all three of them were as perfectly fine as any man could be. Mr. Eddington loved to ride and was fit with a healthy head of brown hair. Mr. Garret fashioned himself a painter and had an artistic mustache to draw attention to his even facial features. Mr. Lovett, being the shortest of the three, had an interest in boating and had a small pleasure vessel docked along the Thames.

Despite there being nothing apparently wrong with them I could not keep myself interested. None of them were Edmund. I could still hear his Irish brogue as he asked if he could kiss me, could still feel the touch of his hands as he cupped my face. But then those visions were replaced by our last meeting. *I shall do my best to pretend we are strangers.*

I shivered and drained the cup of tea I was clutching.

Anne side-eyed me. "Would you like some more?"

I smiled gratefully as she poured me another cup and then topped her own up as well.

"Please, do go on, Mr. Garret," I told the man with the thin and curly mustache. He must spend an inordinate amount of time waxing it into shape.

"As I was saying," he said, motioning with a cracker. "My latest painting will be a part of the revolving exhibit at a gallery in York."

"How wonderful. That is an impressive accomplishment."

"I am glad you think so, Ms. Easton. Perhaps in the future you might let me take you on a trip to York so that you may admire my painting."

"Perhaps," I said vaguely to avoid making promises. It was best to switch subjects. "What about you, Mr. Lovett, when will you go boating next?"

* * *

"That was torture."

Bartley had finally let out the visitors, and Anne and I were free to slouch and lean back into the settee cushioning.

Anne picked up one of the decorative pillows and smacked it against my side. "Tell me about it. Let us agree to not have a repeat of this. I believe I would prefer a simple prearranged marriage over listening to a group of men one-upping each other again."

"Marvelous, I will let John know."

Anne shook her head and laughed. "No, thank you. I do not need any help." She grabbed one of the tarts to munch on and sighed.

"Have you figured out what to do with your family then?" I asked. The sole reason Anne wanted to come to London was to find a husband that would raise her family back up from the clutches of ruin and poverty.

Anne stopped chewing. "Not yet. However," she motioned at the door through which the three suitors had left. "I can no longer pretend to want that."

"Me either. Perhaps I should focus on enjoying the rest of the season. No more men. I have plenty of time to find love, right?"

"Right," Anne said decidedly. "That reminds me of something Mr. Garret said; we should go to an art gallery. There is no need for us to sit here and mope around all day."

"That sounds like a spectacular plan."

Anne swiped crumbs from the side of her mouth. "Do you mind if I invite Willa?"

* * *

A couple of hours later, Anne, Willa, and I found ourselves staring at rows upon rows of paintings at the Watercolor Exhibit on Old Bond Street. A large skylight illuminated the paintings which were hung from ceiling to floor, so tightly fitted against one another that barely any of the red damask wallpaper peeked through. The most well-known artists had their works displayed at eye-level while the lesser-known ones had their works skied. John and Rose had joined us as well. My brother was taking an interest in a beautiful watercolor that depicted the coastline of the English Channel up near Brighton. After a discussion with Rose, he turned to the gallerist, a gray-haired man with a bulbous nose, and asked to purchase it. The gallerist hemmed and hawed until they settled upon a price.

"Well, since I have spent coin already, why not venture out to new Bond Street and spend some more," John remarked. "Would you like to go shopping?"

"Yes." My face brightened. I loved shopping and what better way to take my mind off thinking about the duke.

The gallerist tacked a sold note onto the frame of the painting and waved us out of the Exhibit. The five of us walked the distance to New Bond Street with its enticing five-storied buildings which housed many fashionable shops. We were not the only group out promenading along the raised pavements. Anne, Willa, and I stopped by a hosier for some new stockings and socks while John and Rose shopped at a hatter. After, we reconvened to stop by one of the tea houses.

"Are you feeling better?" Rose asked after pulling me aside when John ordered us all something to drink.

I wanted to say nothing and pretend everything was fine, but Rose gave me a pointed look.

"Beth, I know something has been going on. Why are you not telling me?" Her face turned worried. "Did I do something?"

"No," I spluttered.

"Then what is it? I am concerned about you. Your brother and I have barely seen you, and now, these past few days, I have seen you walking listlessly around the house. If there is something I can do..."

I heaved and glanced at the counter where my brother was still ordering. "Can we speak outside?"

"Of course, I will let John know we will be right back." Rose slipped away and joined John. She slid her hand on his shoulder and whispered something in his ear, punctuated by a kiss on his cheek. My brother nodded and smiled at her.

"What did you tell him?"

"That we were just going outside for a moment and not to wait to drink his tea."

We stepped outside and took a seat at a bench placed near the entrance.

"Tell me," Rose said.

"It truly is nothing to worry about," I said. "The season is just not what I expected."

Rose scanned my face. "I have a feeling that you are not telling me the whole truth. I won't press you for an answer, but I hope you know that you can talk to me. I may be married to your brother now but I was your friend first. I don't know what I would have done without you when I first arrived at Hawthorne."

I laughed. "Those first few days I was certain John would have turned you out onto the streets."

"You are probably right. You were the only thing standing between staying at Hawthorne or sleeping on the side of the road." Rose sighed and tightened her arm around me. "I love you, Beth. Remember that."

I swallowed away the guilt that was gnawing at my conscience. I did want to tell Rose about the duke, but I did not think I was ready. What would I say? I could not promise that it was over because with every beat of my heart I hoped it wasn't.

"I will," I said thickly.

Rose let go of me. "Ready for some tea?"

"Yes. Before it gets too cold."

Rose flashed me a smile. "Well, we can't have that." Softly, she added to herself, "though, I could really go for a latte instead."

John slid out chairs for Rose and me. I sat down and took a sip of tea. Rose added multiple cubes of sugar and a generous helping of cream to hers. She preferred things sweet.

"This was a nice day," I said.

My brother grinned. "And I have a new painting to show for it. Where do you think we should hang it?"

"What about the dining room?" Anne said.

"It would look nice above the buffet table. What do you think, Rose?" I asked.

"That might be a good place. Let's settle on a spot when we are back at Hawthorne." Rose looked at Willa. "You should come visit Westbridge after the season is over. You are more than welcome to stay with us for a couple of weeks or perhaps Anne and her family would love to host you as well."

Anne's face lit up. "I think that is a splendid idea. My brother, Randolph, is currently teaching at Rose's school; I would love to show you around."

Willa's eyes crinkled as she smiled. "I would love that."

17

'William And Susan'

None of the suitors that had shown up to our London town house had made a favorable impression. None of them possessed the conversational skills, wit, or looks I was interested in. I wanted to find my equal; someone who would not bore me to death, who could discuss things that mattered, someone who wanted more than just a pretty wife to hang on his arm.

I wanted...

No.

I gritted my teeth. Edmund was a duke, and I had lied to him; he would never listen to me again. I had not seen him since that night, and while I had been thinking about it, I had not even had the decency to try to apologize again.

I needed something to do to take my mind off things which is why the invitation to a musicale at Mr. And Mrs. Alcott's home came at the perfect time.

The Alcott's daughter, Olivia, was known to be an accomplished pianist, having studied with the well-known Italian Maestro, Marchetti, since she was eight. The musicale would be a rather intimate affair, no more than fifty or so guests. It might be a chance to enjoy the music and mingle with other guests. Plus, I was excited to see Willa again; she had sent a letter to let us know that she was also invited to tonight's soirée.

Anne and I walked about the Alcott's music room, chatting here and there with the other attendees. Every so often the Alcott's butler would announce the arrival of another esteemed guest. It was a rather large room though it still felt cozy with the careful placement of velvet loveseats and mahogany chairs around the room and sumptuous drapes livening up the windows. A refreshment table had been set out in a corner which held a large pitcher of punch. We stopped near a pair of forest green upholstered chairs and decided it would be a good place from which to observe the music. I was wondering when Mr. And Mrs. Alcott's daughter would start playing; so far, she had not made an appearance.

I turned my head. Near the entrance, the butler scraped his throat, readying himself to announce another guest.

"The Duke of Cashel and his companion, Ms. Chapman."

"Edmund," I muttered, as the butler's deep voice faded away. I stood rooted to the spot, staring at the duke's face. I had not expected to see him this evening; we ran in different circles plus there were many events and parties in London during the season I doubted he would ever go to a simple musicale.

Before I could decide whether I should look away or hide,

his gaze turned towards me. His eyes widened slightly when he saw me, his body halting in the entrance. Just when I though my presence did indeed affect him, his face pulled back into that of a bored yet pleasant gentleman and turned towards the companion on his left.

A sour taste flooded my mouth when I saw him speaking with the well-dressed woman, and I could not help but purse my lips. Perhaps I had imagined his slight reaction to me. Perhaps I had been looking for something that was not there. A lazy smile plastered on the Edmund's face as he led the woman to the table of refreshments in the corner of the room. I bit my lip and hastily turned, bumping into Anne a tad too forcefully.

"Careful," she said, rubbing her shoulder.

"I apologize, I did not mean to run into you like that."

"What is wrong?" she started before glancing over my shoulder, understanding appearing in her large brown eyes. "Ah, the duke."

I sighed. "What is he even doing here? And who is that woman he is with?"

Anne gazed at the unknown woman. The duke was holding out a glass of punch towards her, his eyes fixed on the red pendant hanging at her clavicle, the same color as her satin dress. "She looks familiar. But where do I recognize her from." Anne tapped her index finger against her chin.

I hardly listened to Anne's words; blood rushed to my ears seeing the duke's attentiveness to that woman. She giggled and pulled out a fan, lifting it up slowly and waving it in front of her face, drawing the eye once more to her plentiful bosom and the large red pendant affixed above it. I had started to clench my teeth at the sight and had to relax my jaw once I noticed the twinge in my cheek muscles. Only a week ago it had been me that Edmund was laughing with.

Anne whispered in my ear. "I figured it out; that woman is Mary Chapman. I attended a ball with her last season."

I pulled my eyes away from the duke and the woman next to him. "Mary Chapman?" I had never heard that name before.

"Yes, her father turned his profits from a shipping company into real estate and now owns a large portion of the property along the Thames, collecting rent and running places for room and board."

"A merchant," I mused. "I wonder why the duke is escorting her."

"Money talks," Anne said with a shrug. "Mary Chapman has an enormous dowry; all she lacks is a title."

"And marrying a duke could certainly fix that." I swallowed back a bit of extra vitriol. After all, it was not Mary's fault that I was jealous. I did feel sorry for Anne; she was from a good family, but with no money left in their coffers, it was difficult for her to find a good marriage prospect. Not that it seemed to matter as much to her since she had met Willa.

Something else nagged at me, and I chewed my lip. "Why would the duke entertain Mary Chapman if she does not have a title? Could that mean that the duke might not care that I do not either?"

"Beth..."

"I know, it is over between us." Peeking over at Edmund, I sighed. "I deceived him, and he has told me that we would be as strangers from now on. That does not stop me from thinking about him."

A high and clear tinkling noise stopped most conversations. Everyone craned their necks towards the sound. Near the piano forte, Mr. Alcott stood tapping a spoon against his crystal glass.

"Welcome everyone this fine evening," he hummed in a smooth baritone. Mr. Alcott extended his arm and pointed towards a slight wisp of a girl with curled brown hair sliding onto the piano bench. "Let me introduce my daughter Olivia. Please enjoy the refreshments while she plays." Olivia kept her eyes downcast, not daring to make eye contact with anyone in the room. However, as soon as she splayed her long fingers across the keys her demeanor changed, as if the world around her disappeared, leaving behind only the music. I thought Rose was an excellent pianist, but when the first notes rang out beneath Olivia's touch, I could have mistaken Rose's skill for that of a beginner.

Next to me, Anne's face brightened as her head swiveled back. I followed her gaze. Willa had entered the room and sneaked up behind us. She slid in between us and greeted Anne with a wide, toothy grin. Willa looked beautiful in a gauzy green dress that accentuated her soft curves.

"Given up on dressing down?" I joked.

Willa shrugged with a wink. "No need to, now that the situation with the duke has been resolved."

I snorted when Willa twirled in her dress. "Your father must have been thrilled to see you off this evening."

"Papa was happy to see me dress nicely." Willa nodded

with a wistful smile. "Though he kept asking what the occasion was."

"Are you not worried he will find you another suitor?"

Willa's smile widened. "I will deal with that when it happens. Now..." She grasped Anne's hand first then also clasped mine before pulling us both away from the sideline. "Let us dance." We joined up with other guests in the middle of the room.

Olivia had transitioned into an energetic Scottish reel so now we were skipping along the floor in time with the music, hooking elbows with each other before moving on to the next dance partner.

While dancing a turn, I noticed the duke still standing near the refreshment table, his head lowered towards Mary Chapman. For the moment, I was glad he had not joined the dance floor. It would be terribly awkward to dance in such close quarters with him. My face must have fallen because next thing I knew Willa hooked her arm with mine and swung me around.

"Forget him," she said, her face lofty and self-assured. "Who wants to marry a duke anyway, terribly boring lot, you know."

I snorted and rolled my eyes before flashing Willa a smile. "Is that right?"

"Of course, it is an established fact that if you are in possession of a title, you then have to be incredibly dull. Cause and effect; just look at my father," Willa added, winking.

Anne overheard Willa's words and smirked like a cat who had gotten cream. "Oh, so that is why I feel so tired whenever you are around."

Willa looked at Anne in mock affront but her eyes sparkled with mirth. "I beg your pardon. It is only the men who are droll. Well..." Willa scrunched up her nose. "And the Duchess of Howe, and Viscountess Harriet, and... Alright, fine, you win this one," Willa told Anne. "But I am excluding myself from the list; my personality is exemplary."

Anne shook her head and laughed. "I will grant you that. There is never a dull moment whenever you are around."

At the piano forte, Olivia transitioned into *Robin Adair* before Mr. Alcott opened up the floor for requests.

"Do we have any singers amongst us?" he said, smiling and glancing around the room. A girl stepped forward, her head bobbing with the weight of her scarfs and other hair adornments. She whispered something to Mr. Alcott and was ushered to stand next to the piano forte.

Once Olivia played the first notes, the girl started singing in a high, clear voice.

"Meet me by moonlight alone, and then I will tell you a tale. Must be told by the moonlight alone in the grove at the end of the vale—"

My attention was pulled away from the singing by an annoying giggling in the corner; Mary Chapman fawning over Edmund. What aggravated me even more was that he did not seem displeased by the attention.

"—You must come for I said I would show the night flowers their Queen Nay turn not away thy sweet head. This the loveliest ever was seen oh! Meet me by the moonlight alone."

I only caught snippets of the lyrics as I watched Mary spill some of her punch down the front of her dress and Edmund pull a cream handkerchief from his pocket and pat at the wet stain on the woman's bosom. Mary took the opportunity to thrust her breasts ever closer to his face.

Anne moved into my line of sight. "Ignore them."

"How can I when that...that woman keeps flaunting her bosom in the duke's face."

Anne grabbed my wrist. "Come let us stand in the other corner and listen to the song. The girl is an accomplished singer."

The change of position did not matter. The room was cozy; therefore, I was aware of everything the duke did— every simpering word, every smile, and laugh. I felt a stab in my heart every time I heard his throaty chuckle. How could he be courting Mary Chapman as if nothing had happened between us.

"Would anyone else like to have a go?" Mr. Alcott said.

I raised my hand. "I would like to go next."

"Beth, what are you doing?" Anne hissed.

I was showing the duke what he was missing. I strutted towards the piano and planted myself next to Olivia.

"What would you like to sing?" the brunette asked. "I can play most popular tunes."

"Do you know *William and Susan*?"

Olivia nodded. "Whenever you are ready."

My singing might not have been of the same caliber as the previous girl, but I had a solid voice nonetheless. I steeled myself and sang the first verse, which was joined by the other spectators, in what I hoped appeared as confidence. Every so often I would glance in Edmund's direction to see if he was paying attention, but Mary Chapman had molded herself to his side, and he was basking in the attention. The crowd clapped and sang along with the lyrics, but none of it mattered to me. I finished the song as evenly as I could and returned to Anne and Willa. Another singer joined Olivia; a burly man this time who burst into a favorite Scottish song.

"Do you mind if we go?" I looked at Anne, pleading. She seemed hesitant, most likely because she wanted to spend more time with Willa.

After moments pause, she said, "Of course." She turned to Willa. "I apologize for leaving early, but I hope we can see each other again soon."

18

Visiting The Duke Of Cashel

Seeing the duke at the dance with Mary Chapman had left a tightness in my stomach, part indigestion and part something I did not quite want to acknowledge. I knew that if I confessed it to Anne, she would say I was jealous. I sighed and flopped around on the mattress, pulling the cover over my face. Oh, who was I fooling? It was jealousy, plain and simple. The thought of Edmund on the arm of another woman left a sour taste in my mouth, and now I could not close my eyes without picturing him in a too familiar embrace with a simpering Mary. A peaceful sleep after the night's event promised to be elusive.

How difficult could it be to find the person you were meant to be with? My brother had found Rose; she practically fell into his lap. And William had traveled to the future with Austin. Why couldn't it be easy for me?

My mind raced back to my courtship with Mr. Danby. I could not always trust my own judgement; the past had proven that. While I had fashioned myself in love, he had turned out to be a crook only out for my dowry.

However, my situation with the duke was not the same; I was older and—I would like to think—a bit wiser. I was not going into this starry-eyed without understanding the consequences. There was not going to be another secret elopement. I wanted, no, I needed a chance to explain myself to the duke, to lay all my cards out on the table. And if he chose to spurn me? So be it. At least I would have been honest about my feelings, even if I needed to cry about it afterwards.

Regardless of the outcome, this sensation, this pull towards one another could not possibly be one-sided. His interest in me while I was still pretending to be Willa was clear, at least to me. I would be sorely mistaken if our mutual attraction turned out to be faked.

Tomorrow, I told myself, tomorrow I would go visit the duke.

* * *

My hands were clammy as I rode the carriage to the Duke of Cashel's London home. Anne, sitting primly beside me, squeezed one hand reassuringly.

While she disagreed with my plan to confess to Edmund, she still supported my decision.

"We are nearly there," she said, taking a peek out of the carriage window.

We stopped in front of a sprawling Palladian style house in the heart of the fashionable Mayfair district, the size of which could have fit the town house my brother was renting about thrice over.

A little flustered, I turned to Anne. "How do I look?"

She stifled a grin and brushed a stray hair away from my face. "Take a deep breath and calm yourself." Anne inhaled with me to calm my nerves.

The carriage driver opened the door. "Ready, misses?"

Anne nodded to the man. "Just a moment." She turned back to me, draped my ponytail, which had been curled into a corkscrew, over my right shoulder and smiled. "You look beautiful. Now, let us go and surprise the duke."

We scrambled out of the carriage and straightened ourselves. I had debated what to wear before eventually settling on my favorite; a cornflower blue dress which, according to Rose, brought out my eyes. I wondered briefly what Rose and my brother would say if they were aware that I was headed to the home of a duke uninvited, before I decided to raise my chin and barrel forward lest I would come to my senses and return home.

"Wait for me," Anne said, as she hurried to catch up. I strode decidedly up the steps of the large home and knocked on the door. After a few minutes, the door creaked open, revealing a well-groomed man in a butler's uniform.

"May I help you, miss?" the butler asked.

I scraped my throat before answering. "My friend, Anne Blakeley, and I came to call on the Duke of Cashel." Despite the relatively cool spring day, my cheeks burned.

"I am afraid the duke is not here," the butler said, his eyes scrutinizing us. My face fell a bit. I had been building up how the meeting with the duke might go. I imagined I would follow a butler into the duke's study, where he would be sitting behind his desk looking ever so serious, and I would confess to him, regardless of the consequences. However, in none of my imaginations had there been a scenario where the duke was away.

"When is the duke expected back?" I asked, showing a hint of urgency in the way I tumbled out the words.

"I would not presume to know, miss. If you have business with the duke, I recommend sending a letter to his estate in Ireland. He has chosen to remain there this season."

"What?" I said utterly confused. Next to me, Anne gasped, an incredulous expression plastered across her face. I must have been making the same ridiculous face.

"As I said," the butler continued, "The Duke of Cashel can be reached at his estate in Ireland."

"The duke is not in London?" I asked to confirm once more. "The duke has not been in London the entire social season?"

"That is correct, miss." The butler nodded. "Now, if that is all, I shall return to my duties."

"Oh, yes, of course." I had inched forward to peek into the house, so now I shuffled back to give the butler the space to close the door.

"Good day to you," the butler said, leaving Anne and I perplexed on the front step.

Anne shook her head. "I do not know what to say. I…" Her words faltered.

I tried to think of an explanation, any scenario that would

make sense. "Do you think the butler could be mistaken? Perhaps the duke is staying somewhere else?"

Anne scrunched up her face as she thought. "Why would he? And if he did, why would he not have sent word to his staff here? His butler was under the impression that the duke was in Ireland. It does not make any sense." Anne and I walked down the steps. She hesitated before spitting out, "What if the duke we have met was an impostor?"

"But he was in London to finalize an engagement with Willa; that surely cannot be faked." I pointed out. "How would he know who to target?"

Anne sighed and pursed her lips. "No, I suppose not, although... I remember the gossip from the night of the ball. I overheard Mrs. Devon and Mrs. Tulley chatting about the duke and what a good prospect he might make for their daughters. They mentioned that he was a bit of a recluse, rarely venturing away from his country estate. That, although he was reported to be handsome, hardly anyone had seen him in person. Both women were excited to see the duke in the flesh."

"Then, it might be easy to impersonate him," I said with a heaviness that echoed in my heart. What was the truth behind the man I had fallen in love with? Had I been deceived again? Perhaps I had learned nothing from my ordeal with Mr. Danby. "I am a fool," I bit out.

"You could not have known."

"I should have listened to you from the start. If I had followed your advice, none of this would have happened."

"He fooled everyone."

My throat constricted. Anne's soft-spoken words only

made it harder to keep my eyes from tearing up. "I want to go home," I croaked out.

"Yes, we will return to the house and fetch you something to drink." Anne hailed a carriage back to the townhouse. We sat in silence during the return, the only sounds the creaking of the wood and the clattering of the wheels as they turned along the many cobblestone streets. My emotions were getting the better of me, and I was worried that if I spoke, I would not be able to hold back the flood of tears that were welling up inside of me.

Back at the home, Anne left me in the sitting room while she went to order some tea. I stood listlessly in the middle of the room, unsure of what to do.

"Are you alright?" Rose walked up behind me. "Is something going on?" I was not certain why but as soon as I heard Rose's gentle voice, I could not hold the tears back any longer. Big fat drops spilled down my cheeks and blurred my vision.

"No, I am not," I heaved. Rose pulled me into a hug.

"Oh Beth, what's going on? You can tell me anything." She tightened her arms around me while I cried on her shoulder.

"I think I loved him," I confessed in between sobs.

Rose patted my back. "Loved who?"

"The duke... at least, I thought he was a duke."

"And now?" Rose tried her best to comfort me, but it was evident that she was confused by my words.

"I do not know." I wiped my nose with the back of my hand, tears soaking Rose's shoulder. Anne entered, followed by a maid who carried a pot of tea. Rose motioned the maid towards the table before brushing my cheek.

"Come, let's sit down and rustle you up a cup of tea." She

ushered me towards the settee and handed me a handkerchief. I blew my nose, which by now had turned a shade of bright red that rivaled that of a ripe tomato. "Here, let's get some liquids into you," Rose said, handing me a cup of fragrant amber liquid. I took a shaky sip of the tea. Once Rose saw I had calmed down a bit, she turned to Anne. "Now, perhaps one of you can explain what happened? I only managed to catch a few words."

Anne gaped at Rose, her eyes flashing to me while she fidgeted with a lace applique on her dress.

"I'm only worried," Rose pushed. "I'm sure John would be too if he'd seen your face earlier. What happened? Did someone do something? Perhaps if you'd tell us we could help?"

I wanted to groan. John would be so angry with me. He had already been difficult to persuade to let me join the social season this year. If he found out about this, he might never let me go anywhere by myself again.

"You cannot tell John," I shot out, pleading.

Rose paused, looking pained. "Beth... I married your brother. I won't keep secrets from him. But I think you don't give him enough credit. John loves you, as do I. We both want what is best for you. Please trust me, you can tell us anything."

I hesitated, the words sticking in the back of my throat. I did not want to let my brother down. Tipping the cup, I finished the dregs of tea, savoring any moment I had before I faced Rose and told her what had happened.

"When Anne and I attended Lady Westham's ball, I helped a friend who did not want to meet the man she was supposed to get betrothed to. I pretended to be her and danced with the duke in her stead." Rose's eyebrows crawled up towards her hairline; her shocked expression would have been funny if it had not been for the circumstances.

"You what?... A duke?" Rose's eyes flashed between Anne and me. "And this friend, I suppose you mean Willa?"

"Yes." I nodded. "The duke assumed I was Willa, and we kept up the ruse for a few weeks before he found out that I was not his soon-to-be betrothed."

"And then?" Rose stood and paced the room. She stopped at the whiskey decanter but sighed and returned to the table to finish the rest of her tea. Anne was focusing her eyes on a random spot on her lap, making sure to not glance at Rose.

"He spurned me."

"Okay..." Rose's eyes were flitting back and forth while she thought. "Are you alright? Does anyone else know?"

I shook my head. "No one."

Rose sighed. "Oh Beth, I'm sorry that happened. But since he was supposed to marry someone else perhaps it's for the best? Maybe you can go to other events and just enjoy the rest of the season. There is always next year. You deserve to find someone who understands the real you and loves you for who you are."

"Will you tell John?"

Rose's shoulders rose as she inhaled. "I won't, but I think you should tell him yourself."

"I will."

"Tell me what?" John said as he strode into the room.

Anne nudged me. I was aware of what she was thinking; I had not told Rose the full truth.

I gave Anne a swift shake of my head. "Later," I whispered.

John kissed his wife's cheek, a bright smile livening up his face. "Did you tell them the good news?"

"What's the good news?" I asked as Rose smiled up at John, her eyes glossy.

Rose pulled her eyes away from John and chuckled. "I hadn't gotten to that, yet. I wanted to wait to do it together. But since we are all here." She paused as she brushed the palm of her hand along her belly. "We're having a baby."

"Really?" I looked at my brother. "I'm going to be an aunt?"

John beamed. "Yes, Rose is pregnant."

I jumped up and kissed Rose's cheek before pulling my brother in for a hug, squeezing him tightly.

"I am so happy for you both. I cannot wait to meet my niece or nephew."

The good news about Rose's pregnancy had managed to subvert my own thoughts and feelings regarding the duke who may or may not be a duke, for most of the day. It was only when Anne pulled me aside in the evening as I prepared to retire that I was forced to confront the strange situation outside the Duke of Cashel's London home once more.

"Why did you not tell Rose everything?" Anne whispered in the corridor. We were standing at the base of the staircase. I heard Rose and John giggle to each other from the sitting room, and, towards the back of the house, the soft tinkling of chinaware and glass as they were being hand washed by a scullery maid.

I lowered my voice as well. "I did not want to omit any-thing, but before I tell Rose and my brother anything more, I need to be certain. Perhaps there is a reason why he has not visited his own home."

"Like what?" Anne raised her brow.

"Well...I do not know, but that does not mean there could not be a reason. A reason I intent to find out."

"Perhaps you should forget about the duke. Rose is right, we can still enjoy the social events this season and perhaps you will find a match next year." Anne held still as she looked at me with anticipation.

"Perhaps," I answered.

Anne let out a weary sigh. "I suppose that will have to do for now."

19

⚭

A Few Old Fish Crates

I was aware that Anne would have preferred it if I had put my thoughts of the duke aside and returned to circle the ballroom floor with her at whatever was the current fashionable location to be, but I could not. I needed to know the truth.

Therefore, the next evening, I remained home while my brother, Rose, and Anne headed out to attend a soirée at the home of a retired naval captain who used to be acquainted with my parents. Though Anne was reluctant to leave me behind.

Across town, there was another event going on, some festivities organized by a wealthy merchant, a good place for other merchants, bankers, and possible investors to meet and mingle. I wagered that Ms. Chapman might be attending, and therefore, there was a good chance that the duke would make an appearance as well.

I pulled a pair of trousers from my dresser drawer and

mumbled a silent thanks to Rose for insisting on having them made. Wearing those in addition to a shirt and a cloak with a hood would make it difficult to recognize me in the dark. The moon was at its smallest, so there would be hardly any light to reveal my appearance.

I did not want to leave prematurely, so I picked at my food, too nervous to eat in earnest. My gaze kept darting back to the standing clock in the kitchen until, finally, I decided it was time to go. With John, Rose, and Anne gone, there was no one to watch my movements, so I pulled on one of the cloaks and drew the hood up over my face before exiting the front door.

* * *

Sticking to the shadows, I waited outside the merchant's alley near the docks. The night was dark with only a smattering of stars visible through the heavy layer of clouds. I kept my eyes focused on the entrance to the warehouse. Soft giggles and murmured voices floated out with the gentle notes of music. Lots of people showed up to celebrate the opening of the new facility. All I had to hope was that the duke—or whomever he was—was in attendance and would be heading home soon. Golden light flickered out of the side windows, illuminating the immediate area.

I did not want to wait in vain, so I sneaked closer and jetted off to a side alley when the last stragglers standing outside the building left. The side windows were high and narrow. I stood on my tiptoes but could not reach them. By Jove, how was I supposed to glance inside and ascertain whether or not the duke was in attendance. I squinted my eyes and searched around the alley. Discarded in a corner, I found a few old fish crates. The sour smell wafting out from them was overwhelming, but I bit back bile and picked them up. Below one of the windows, I stacked the crates as securely as I could. Grabbing on to the brick wall, I climbed up on the crates. I held my breath for a moment as the wooden slats creaked, groaned, and wobbled, but against all odds, they were able to hold my weight. I exhaled and peeked through the window, scanning the crowd. Where was the duke?

Groups of people gathered near a long table covered in a cloth that reached the floor, laden with treats and bowls of punch. I focused on each of the faces, but none of them was the duke. Disappointed, I moved my attention elsewhere, but I did not see him dancing in the middle either. I was about to give up hope when I spotted a dark-haired figure in the corner. My heart raced. So, I was right; the duke was here.

I carefully lowered myself to the ground and returned to my earlier vantage point. There, hidden in darkness, I leaned against the wall and waited for the duke to exit.

It was nearly midnight when I spotted him leaving the warehouse. He lowered his head at that insipid Mary Chapman before heading in the direction of the Thames.

I had been expecting him to hail a cab so I had to scramble to follow him. Though for my first time out following someone, I thought I was doing a splendid job. I wished I could tell Anne about it later, but I doubted that she would be thrilled that I left the house by myself to follow a man who we knew for a fact had been lying about his identity. And all that in the middle of the night. What was I doing? Had I gone mad?

But as they said; in for a penny, in for a pound. It was too late to turn back now.

I planted my feet as quietly as I was able while trailing Edmund who, twenty or so feet in front of me, walked without a care in the world, even whistling a merry tune. My heart pounded. I did not want to confront him so near the water; it was better to find out where he was going first.

Wait, where did he go? I only took my eyes off him for a moment. I picked up my pace and sighed a breath of relief when I found him around the corner in front of a flight of stairs. He walked up to the second story and, after unlocking the door, entered a room.

Not needing to hide for the moment I walked to the front of the building. A large sign was tacked up in the ground floor window; *Rooms for Let, 10 Shillings a Week.*

So, this was where Edmund was staying.

I swallowed back my apprehension, climbed the flight of stairs to the fake duke's room, and knocked.

Edmund opened the door and froze at the sight of me, his jaw dropped.

"What—what are you doing here?" He darted forward to peer over the side of the stairs.

"It is only me," I said before realizing that perhaps that might not have been the smartest move. One of many not very smart moves I had made since my arrival in London.

Edmund stepped back again, clearly relieved no one else was there. "That still does not answer my question, Beth. Why are you here?"

"Should I not ask you what you are doing here instead,

Your Grace?" I emphasized the last part enough for Edmund —or whatever his name was—to widen his eyes as understanding flooded his face.

He moved aside, creating space for me to enter. "Perhaps we should speak inside." I followed him into the room. He turned to me. "So, what is it you want to say?"

I unfastened the cloak I was wearing and deposited it on top of a chair before crossing my arms. "I went to the Duke of Cashel's London home to apologize for my deceit when I came to find out, to my surprise, that the duke was not in London. In fact, he never left Ireland." I paced and stared at the man in front of me. "This made me wonder; who, then, was the man that I spent all those days with, if he was not the duke."

"You were not supposed to find out."

"Find out what? Who you are? You acted as if I had committed a sin when you found out I was not lady Willa Balfour. And I admit, I felt guilty. But you have been doing the same thing, and for what? What is it that you are doing?" My blood was boiling at his hypocrisy. "You made me feel horrible that day at the Farnsby's ball, and for what?"

Edmund—or whatever his name was—paled. "I had no other option."

"No other option?" I scoffed at him.

He shook his head. "When I found out that you were not Willa, and even before if I am being frank, I knew I needed to distance myself from you. My life is complicated."

His words offered no explanation. I needed more. "Why? What are you doing here?"

"I am here to do what I did that day I took you to visit the orphanage."

"What does the orphanage have to do with anything? What do I even call you?"

The man who I had thought was the duke chewed his lip. "You can call me Henry Fielding, though I am more widely known under a different nom du guerre.

I blinked, confused, waiting for…Henry…to elaborate.

Henry pointed at the door. "You should leave, return to your safe world of dances and cream tea with ladies. I am so close to what I set out to do."

"Which is? I want to know who you are. I am not leaving until I do."

Henry smacked his fist against the wall and cursed. "Fine, you want to know who I am? Perhaps you have heard of the Gentleman Thief?"

I gasped. "You mean to say that he is…you?" I did know that name, as most people in England did; the bane of the ton and folk hero to those in need. He swindled riches from those unscrupulous few with deep pockets and divided it amongst those in need. Of course, it meant that the law was always searching for him. The Gentleman Thief had been there the day William stood trial, though I had not paid attention to his appearance then. If I had, perhaps I would have realized his identity from the start.

His brown eyes stared into mine. "He and I are one and the same. Now that you know the truth, I need you to leave. And if you could promise me one thing; forget that I am here. Mary Chapman and her father have hurt a lot of people on their way to the top. A bit of wealth distribution would be the least of what they deserve."

I frowned at his insistence at throwing me out of his room. His short explanation was not nearly enough; I needed more.

I stomped my feet. "No, I am not leaving."

"What is it that you are looking for?" Henry asked, his real name still foreign in my head. His gaze darkened and his expression turned almost feline as he prowled towards me. Instinctively, I backed up until I knocked my shoulder against the wall of the cramped rental room. I gasped as he closed the distance and pushed his firm body against me, our faces near enough for me to feel his breath warming my skin. I was uncertain whether I wanted to kiss the scoundrel or call for help. Perhaps it was a bit of both.

"Is it this?" His hand traced slowly along the side of my body until it reached my hip then he bunched the fabric up and lifted the hem of my shirt. I shivered from the brisk air reaching my bared stomach. "Are you a spoiled girl who wants to experience a bit of adventure? Take a break from society?"

"It is not like that" I lifted my chin. "Why are you trying to push me away?"

"What is it like then?" Henry bit back.

He was angry, yes. But beyond that, I sensed a sadness. I wondered what it was. I knew I should leave and never think of this man again, but my body betrayed me. My skin felt like it was on fire.

"I switched identities to help a friend."

"A friend?" Henry raised his brow and scoffed. "I am sure you did not mind it when you thought you were being courted by a duke."

"I do not care about titles; I never have." I pushed my palms against his chest.

"No?" He lowered his face towards mine until our noses skimmed, a dark glimmer in his eyes. I needed only to move a hairsbreadth and those soft, firm lips would be pressed against mine. A sliver of a smile crossed Henry's lips as he saw the struggle in my eyes. "That is what I thought. The lady is too proud to slum it with the likes of me."

"Stop it, Edmund." I raised my chin and stared fiercely back at him.

Dropping the hem of my shirt and stepping back, he said, "I am not Edmund."

"I know that. Despite what you may think, I still care. You cannot tell me that everything we have experienced these past weeks has been a lie. I refuse to believe that."

"What does it matter? You can run safely back to your family. Perhaps find one of those other dandies to marry you. You would never consider cavorting with the likes of me."

"The likes of you? And what would that be? A man who helps those in need? A man who is kind and generous to everyone who deserves it?"

Henry's face twisted as he turned away from me. "A bastard, a thief, a liar." I fell silent as his words echoed through the room. He shot out a sad laugh. "I told you, you would not like the person I am."

I went over to him, cupped his face, and standing on my tiptoes, planted a kiss on his lips. "I like you just fine."

Henry's eyes widened momentarily before closing. He snaked his arm around me and pulled me in tight, nipping at my lower lip before crushing his mouth against mine. I sighed against him and deepened our kiss, my hands wandering around his muscular back. Henry's tongue worked its way inside my mouth, teasing and tasting. His hands slid lower until they reached my buttocks. I yelped as he gripped my thighs firmly and lifted me up until my legs were practically wrapped around his waist.

Henry made me feel vulnerable and very much alive. How scandalized my brother and all the people of the ton would be if they could see me now.

Henry never once stopped his onslaught of kisses as he carried me the few steps towards the narrow single bed. He deposited me on top of the grayish blanket and took a moment to look at me. My cheeks flushed as I imagined the sight he was seeing. My shirt raised and rumpled to just below my breasts, hair wild, and lips swollen from his kisses. I moved my hand to lower my shirt.

"Don't," Henry said. "Let me look at you." His appreciative gaze slid down the length of me. "You are so lovely, a mhuirnin." He moved to sit on the bed. "Can I touch you?"

I nodded before swallowing. "As long as I can, too?"

Henry grinned, his canines showing. "Anywhere you might like, love."

I started with running my fingers through his dark hair. He groaned, capturing my lips. Then, Henry licked and nibbled down the curve of my face and neck until he reached my clavicle. I ran my fingers across his shirt, frustrated by the barrier between his skin and myself. Henry caught my frown.

"Would you like it off?"

I licked my lips. "Yes."

With a sweep of his arm, he tugged the cream shirt up and

over his head, revealing a sharp chest and a fascinating trail of hairs that ran down from his belly button until it disappeared behind the edge of his trousers. I grazed my fingertips along the hairs.

I had never done anything like this before. Even my ill-begotten dalliance with Mr. Danby had only existed of longing gazes and the odd kiss on the top of my hand. Now, heat pooled at the apex of my thighs as Henry kissed my skin ever lower. His right hand palmed the side of my breast as if he was deciding on which plump fruit to pick, his thumb skimming the peak of my breast and turning my nipples into hard pebbles. Here and there, he stopped to mutter in Irish. The sounds were attractive but unintelligible to my ears.

Henry's right leg rested between my legs providing a sweet kind of pressure. I wanted more. More of this feeling. More of him.

"What do I do? I-I never," I confessed.

Henry stilled and broke his kiss to look at me.

"Should I undress?"

Some undefinable emotion crossed Henry's face and he groaned, pushing himself up from me.

"What is wrong?"

Henry sat down at the edge of the bed and turned his head away. "You are an innocent debutante. We cannot do this. You should return home, return to your own social circles without being ruined."

I reached for his shoulder, but he shrugged it off and stood. Blanching, I pulled down the hem of my shirt. As for my disheveled hair and kiss-swollen lips, there was nothing I could do.

Tears pricking behind my eyes as I said, "I thought you wanted me, too."

"Do not be naive," Henry shot out.

The barb hit its intended target. My chest contracted in pain. What a pretty little fool I was to be taken in twice by such villainous men. The last of the heat left my body until my limbs turned to ice.

"I shall go then," I said flatly.

"You should." Henry resembled a pillar the way he stood stiff and rigid beside the bed; his face pulled into an emotion-less mask. What had happened? Only moments ago, I had been teasing my fingers along the skin on his still bare chest. I scrambled off the bed and swiped my hands across my wild hair in an effort to smooth it back into some semblance of propriety.

Henry's gaze seemed disconnected as if he was trying his hardest not to see me. "Do not come looking for me again. With any luck, we will not find each other at the same social events while I finish what I started. Soon I will return to Ireland and you shall forget I ever even existed."

I snatched my cape from the chair in a huff. "You are discarding me so you can dance and flirt with that Mary Chapman. I saw you all over her at Mrs. Alcott's musicale."

"And what if I was," he said, his voice almost bored. "My business with Ms. Chapman is my own."

I touched my fingers to my sore lips. "Your own...Yes, I suppose it is." I threw the cape around my shoulders and stomped towards the door. "I wish I never met you," I hurled at Henry as I exited the room.

"As you wish," Henry whispered behind me, but I was too

angry to stop and glance back. I hurried down the steps, burying my face in the depths of my hood, hoping no one should notice my departure.

20

The Gentleman Thief

"Covent Garden, please."

I managed to procure a hackney cab, though the driver gave me a strange look when he heard my voice.

"Tis an odd time for a woman to be out by herself." His eyes flashed from my face to my trousers.

"I need to go home. Will you take me?" I pulled out coin from my pocket and held it up to his face.

His eyes flitted back to my face and after a long considering sniff, he snatched the money from my hands and stuffed it into his satchel. His long, thin fingers patted the worn leather after he closed it. With a huff, the driver jumped down from the driver's seat and opened the carriage door. The soft glow from the streetlamps glinted off the man's short silver beard.

"None o' my business where ye are going, miss. Get yerself in."

Darkness swallowed me up as I entered the cabin and

perched myself on the slim bench. The lack of light suited me just fine. I did not want to think about what had happened with Edmund—no, Henry—just now, but my mind kept replaying every moment. I touched my fingers to my lips, still sore from his kisses. Did I really let him carry me to bed even after finding out who he was? He did not take it any further, of course. I suppose I should be glad for that. What had I been thinking? By Jove, he was a criminal. Perhaps one who did more good than bad but a criminal nonetheless.

A criminal who had stolen my heart...

And despite me knowing the truth, he had still turned me away. I had really done it now. All I could hope for was that my family was still out when I got home. I did not want to have to explain my late-night absence.

The black cab jostled as it turned onto another street, and I was left contemplating the choices I had made until the wheels creaked to halt and we stopped at the side of the road near Covent Garden. From there, it was only a short walk back to the house John was renting.

"Be safe, miss," the driver said with a tip of his black hat. I nodded and stepped onto the pavement. With a snap of his reins, the hackney cab driver shot off into the night, on his way to find another paying customer.

Shivering in the cool night air, I rubbed my arms to improve my circulation. The stench of the day market still lingered, rotting vegetables and the accumulated excrement of horses providing a heady, unpleasant smell. The manure would not be removed until the crack of dawn when young urchins swept the streets. Somewhere, an owl hooted, breaking through the silence.

I walked the few streets back to the house we were staying. At first glance, I could not detect any light seeping from the windows. John, Rose, and Anne could still be at the dance, or they could already be asleep. Regardless, I would have to be careful. Letting myself in through the side gate, I sneaked up to the house and entered through the servants' entrance. Soft snores reverberated through the hallway as I crept past the servants' bedrooms.

I managed to get all the way up to the second floor where Anne and my bedrooms were located without incident. I stood outside Anne's door and held my breath as I listened for any sounds that might tell me she was inside, but there were none.

My chest squeezed. I had hoped Anne was home; I wanted my friend. With a sigh, I undid the cloak and returned to my room.

I threw the cloak over the side of my vanity stool and moved on to unbuttoning my trouser, my hand skimming along the patch of skin beneath my navel. I paused and repeated the motion with my finger, drawing loose figure eights.

Henry had touched me there, and...I slid my hand up past the side of my breast, stopping at my clavicle. There. When I closed my eyes, I could still feel the sensation of his hot breath against my flesh. How my skin tingled wherever he touched me.

The Gentleman Thief had not been very gentlemanly then.

I shook my head to cast out the images of Henry and myself in multiple stages of undress. We were over; he had turned me away. Though part of me wondered if he had pushed me away to protect me. He was a wanted man, after all.

I continued unbuttoning my trousers and pulled them off. Next, I removed my shirt, replacing my day clothes with a night gown. When Anne did finally return home, I was brushing out my snarled hair.

Her light and quick steps danced across the old, creaking floor until she reached her bedroom. I dropped the brush onto my vanity and shot out the door.

"Anne."

Her hand reached for the doorknob, but she dropped it to her side when she heard my voice and turned towards me.

"I imagined you would be asleep by now. Did I wake you? I was trying to be quiet." Her face was bright and slightly flushed. She looked happy.

"You did not wake me." I bounced forward and pulled her into a hug. She leaned into my grip, resting her chin against my shoulder.

"What is that for?" she asked, her voice muffled by my hair.

"I am glad you have returned. Now...tell me, how was your night?"

"How about I tell you while I take down my hair?" Anne opened the door to her room and sat down at her vanity. She raised her hands and pulled at a section of curls pinned together against her scalp.

"Let me." I stepped behind her and grabbed the pin, gently teasing it out of her hair.

Anne sighed and seemed to sink into the chair. "That feels so much better." She kicked off her pink slippers beneath the vanity. One dark curl fell to the side of her face. I moved on to the other pins.

"Your brother and Rose danced almost the entire evening.

I overheard a couple of matrons gossiping about it. Apparently, it is uncouth to only dance with your wife; he was supposed to give some of the eligible ladies a chance to shine also." Anne raised her brow and smirked.

I rolled my eyes at her and laughed. "John has no interest in following the advice of society mothers. That ended once he married Rose." I worked another pin out of Anne's hair and dropped it on a small dish on top of her vanity.

Anne glanced down at her elegant hands; the tips of her ears reddened. I wondered what she was thinking, but before I could ask, she said, "The place we went to this evening had an orangerie, so Willa and I sneaked away from the dancing to explore." Anne paused and reddened even further; she looked up shyly, our eyes meeting in the mirror. "We were the only ones there, and she kissed me on the cheek."

"Did you want her to?"

Anne nodded. "I think I did." She swallowed. "Yes, but what does it mean?"

"Did you ask Willa what it meant?"

"I-no." Anne turned her head to look up at me. "Should I have?"

I patted Anne on the crown of her head as I fished out the last of the pins and let down her full head of dark curls. "What do you want it to mean?"

Anne chewed the corner of her fingernail. "I do not know. I...like Willa." She spat out the words as if with great effort, swiveling around in her seat. "But there is my family to consider; Mary, Randolph, and Mama, they are relying on me. I set out to find someone to marry me this season. Your brother so graciously offered to sponsor me and even offered to provide a dowry, and now…and now, I feel conflicted." Worry lines etched into her marble forehead. "I do not know what to do, and I am not certain of what Willa wants either."

"Perhaps you can ask what Willa wants. However, when it comes down to your family, you are not alone. Who knows, there might still be another solution that does not involve marriage with a random man."

Anne pursed her lips and pointed her finger at my chest. "And what about you? What are you going to do?"

My eyes darted to the side, avoiding Anne's assessing stare.

"Will you stop thinking about that man, whoever he is?"

"The Gentleman Thief," I answered before I could stop myself.

Anne's eyes rounded, her mouth turning into a perfect circle. "Wait…what?"

I scrambled. "Nothing, it is nothing."

"No, it is not nothing." She crossed her arms. "That is why you wanted a hug. You went to see him tonight, am I right? Is that why you stayed home to begin with? To sneak out and confront him? Where did you even find the man? He was not at the real duke's estate."

I lowered my head and looked apologetic. "I made a guess that since he was escorting Mary Chapman at the musicale he might be in attendance at another event where she might be present."

"The opening of the new warehouse near the docks." Anne's voice sounded baffled. "I read that in the papers." Then she narrowed her eyes. "You went there by yourself? Anything could have happened. What were you thinking?"

I wondered that exact thing to myself. "I found him," I told

Anne. "He was renting a room near the Thames. I knocked on his door and demanded he tell me who he was."

Anne's frown deepened, and she stood and walked to her dresser to pour a glass of water.

"He told me his nom de guerre, the Gentleman Thief."

Anne sipped some water. "You should report him to the Bow Street Runners."

"No," I rushed to say. "I will not, I cannot."

"Why in heavens not?" Anne shook her head and set down her glass.

I paced, wearing lines down the floorboards of Anne's bedroom. "It is funny," I said, trailing off. Anne frowned and waited for me to continue. "If I had only paid attention to the other people at the courthouse that day of William's hearing, I would have recognized him from the very start. It is strange to think we have crossed paths before London."

Us meeting felt almost serendipitous, but he had pushed me away again and again. Despite everything, I could not turn him in. Perhaps his methods were not in accordance with the law, but he had a strong sense of righteousness. What he did was to help those in need. I had to commend that. "He is a good person."

"The Gentleman Thief is a criminal. There are warrants out for his arrest." Anne grabbed my arm. "You put yourself in a lot of danger tonight. Who knows what he might have done?" Her eyes scrutinized my face. Blushing, I wondered if she could tell that I had been thoroughly kissed by him.

Anne seemed to think, noticing the redness creeping up my face. "Did he...? Are you?" She asked it gently, monitoring my reaction.

I shook my head. "No."

She let out her breath. "Good."

"He kissed me, but that is all. We did not take things further."

"And you will not report him?"

"No," I said, decidedly. "Despite his lies, he is a good man." Henry might have pushed me away but his intentions were honorable in regards to everything else.

Anne let out a weary chuckle. "Look at the two of us; one has fallen for a thief while the other needs to marry for money but loves someone she cannot marry."

"Love?" I looked up at Anne.

Anne smiled bashfully and shrugged. "I suppose I do."

"Willa is very lucky."

Anne breathed in deeply. "I do not know what to do."

"We will figure out a plan." I glanced at Anne's clothing. She was still wearing the pink satin dress she wore to the dance. "How about you change into your night gown and we heat up some milk?

"Would we not wake the staff?"

I smirked. "When I slipped past their doors earlier, I could hear them snoring. I think, as long as we are quiet, we should be fine."

Anne tutted as she moved to undress herself. "I still cannot believe you went to the docks by yourself in the middle of the night."

"In trousers."

Anne stifled a laugh, her eyes crinkling.

I smiled. "You should have seen the cab driver who took me home when he first heard my voice."

This time, Anne laughed. "Beth, you have no shame." She pulled on her nightgown.

A soft knock sounded on the door. I glanced back to see the door creak open and Rose's face peeking around the corner.

"Hi, I just wanted to check in on you," Rose said, looking at me. "Your room was empty, so I figured you were with Anne."

Anne picked up a hair tie from her vanity. "Come on in. We were going about to go downstairs for some warm milk, if you would like to join?"

"I would like that."

"Would John like to join as well?" Anne's fingers raked her hair and tamed the strands into a braid, tying it off with the tie.

"He's gone to bed. I think we can keep it to us girls." Rose winked.

The three of us, barefooted and dressed in long, flowing nightgowns, descended the staircase as a trio of specters that haunt the darkened halls in a ghost story. We tiptoed past the corridors until we reached the kitchen.

"I will fetch the milk," Anne said, heading for the larder. Rose grabbed a fire poke from its spot on the wall and squatted down in front of the cast-iron hob grate.

"Can you hand me some more coal?"

The leftover coals were smoldering in the bottom of the grate, waiting to be fed additional fuel. Rose poked at the coals, making sure additional oxygen reached the center. I grabbed a handful of coals from the basket and dropped them in as Rose leaned to the side. Small flames licked up the sides of the new, still black coal, casting an orange glow.

Anne returned, heaving a pail of milk and set it down on an open workspace. A while later, we sat down, enjoying three steaming cups of milk that had been heated up on the hob grate.

Rose sighed and brushed her hand along her stomach. "If only I could get *Oreos*. A type of cookie from back home," she clarified. "I've been craving sweets, and they would have gone well with the milk."

"Perhaps John can spoil you and order sweetmeats or ices from *Gunter's Tea Shop*. We could always bring dry sweetmeats like taffy, butterscotch, or sugared almonds back with us when we return to Hawthorne."

"Now that is a bright idea. I will have to ask John in the morning."

21

Gunter's Tea Shop

"Tom, why not let Estelle join you up front?" John said to the driver and stable master. Estelle beamed and scurried to his side, excited to be invited along. Tom held out his hand and helped Estelle up onto the drivers bench on the carriage.

"You really don't mind, sir?" she asked again in her French-accented English, rearranging her skirts until she sat comfortably. "Gunter's is expensive."

John smiled magnanimously. "Not at all, the season is nearly over so let us all enjoy some ices. Perhaps we can even get some sweets to give to the rest of the staff at Hawthorne. I am certain Mrs. Avery and her niece Clara would like some caramels. What do you think Hugh would like?"

"Marzipan."

"Then I shall include some of that as well." John turned to, Anne, Rose, and myself. "Ready, ladies?" He held open the door and let us enter the carriage first. Then, after ensuring Rose was seated, slid in next to her.

Tom stopped the carriage at the east side of Berkley Square. John pulled back the curtains. A variety of people stood outside the confectionery shop, flaunting their ices.

John signaled with his hand and a waiter strutted towards our carriage. "Would you like to place an order?" A layer of sweat lined the man's forehead, and some streaks of beige, pink, and green, marred the front of his apron.

"Six ices, please. Your most popular flavors. And," John pulled a written list and some money notes from his breast pocket, "everything on this list."

The waiter took the money and list from his hand and returned to the shop. Fifteen minutes later, he returned, handing John a parcel. "These are the sweetmeats you've requested. The caramels were sold out, but we can deliver those in a few days."

John nodded and gave the waiter our address. John exited the carriage and helped hand out the ices.

"Should we enjoy them outside?" Rose said, glancing at the other couples eating their cold treats in the sunshine.

"Whatever my wife wants," John said, helping her out onto the street. Anne and I scooted out next.

"Tom, Estelle, enjoy your ices. We shall go for stroll."

I scooped a bite of the cold, creamy concoction into my mouth, the herbaceous notes of lavender hitting my tongue.

"You should try some of mine," Anne said, holding out a spoon towards me. "Orange flower, I believe."

I tried hers. "Delicious."

I had missed days like these, hours spent in pleasant company with my family and friends. I smiled widely as we crossed the street, looking out for traffic. The sun shone down on us, barely a cloud in the sky. The ice cream was refreshing in the summer heat.

"What should we do this evening?" Anne said.

Rose craned her neck back at us, her arm hooked with John's. "The Brocklehursts' did send over an invitation for a game night. I have not given them an answer, yet."

I could not hide my dislike at the mention of the Brocklehursts. I had not forgiven Arabella for her unfortunate appearance at the dance. If it wasn't for her, I could have spoken with...Henry, before my true identity was revealed. Not that he had been honest then.

Still...I was not overly fond of the Brocklehursts. I savored the last few bites of ice cream.

Rose smirked. "I believe the deafening silence speaks volumes. We should find something else to do."

"John Easton, is that you?"

My brother stopped. A gray-haired man carrying a sleek rosewood cane with an embossed brass handle motioned towards John.

"Arthur Devensies, good to meet you. What are you doing at Berkley Square? Last time I saw you, you were starting a practice near Birmingham." He grabbed the man's hand and greeted him. "Let me introduce my wife, Rose Easton, and my sister, Beth Easton, and her friend Ms. Blakeley."

The man inclined his head. "Nice to meet you Mrs. Easton, Ms. Easton, and Ms. Blakeley."

John turned to us. "Mr. Devensies is a solicitor. He was a tremendous help with William's case."

Mr. Devensies shook his head, his eyes sorrowful. "Terrible business, that was, imprisoning an innocent man on such accusations. That blasted Tremblay deserved what happened to him after getting himself indebted and lying to the court. How is Mr. Chambers?"

"He is well. William is traveling abroad."

The solicitor nodded. "It is good to get away, set the mind right again." His eyes focused on John, and he lowered his voice. "Do you remember the other accused at Mr. Chamber's trial?"

"Not much, why?" John's eyes narrowed and seemed to examine Mr. Devensies.

Mr. Devensies' eyes flashed to us. Then he clapped a hand on John's back. "Perhaps we should speak in private for a moment. It is sensitive information and might not be suitable for the ladies' ears."

"It is alright, Devensies. My companions can hear."

Mr. Devensies considered John's words, taking a moment before opening his mouth again. "Alright, however, you will need to keep this to yourselves." He leaned in closer. "I have it on good authority from an inside man at the Bow Street Runners that the Gentleman Thief has been spotted in London. In fact, it is the reason I am here at all."

I gasped, before clapping a hand over my mouth, aware of Anne's pointed stare.

"Yes." Mr. Devensics nodded, appreciating my reaction. Though he had no idea for the reason behind it nor did my brother or Rose. No one but Anne and me knew that the Gentleman Thief had been pretending to be the Duke of Cashel.

"I was hired by a man in Birmingham who recognized the criminal, but alas, we were too late to apprehend him there. We ventured to London under the assumption that we might catch him here during the season. Where else could the gentlemen thief have his pick of the ton?"

"And did you?" I asked, my face paling.

"Are you alright, dear?" Mr. Devensies frowned.

"I am, please, continue," I urged.

"Well, you might recall there was a fairly large bounty on his head." Mr. Devensies looked to John.

"Yes, I recall reading about it in the papers."

Mr. Devensies sniffed and curled his fingers around the cane handle. "My client and I attended many soirées, looking for the thief. We almost believed we had made an error and the criminal had moved on to a different city or town, but then my client was invited to an opening near the docks."

My eyes widened. The docks...that meant the man had attended the opening of the warehouse. The event that Henry attended with Mary Chapman, the one where I had followed him home.

"That is where he found the man dancing with a merchant's daughter."

John lifted his brow. "I was under the impression that the Gentleman Thief only seduces women of the ton?"

"So was I," Mr. Devensies said, adding emphasis to his words. "However, apparently her father has amassed a tremendous amount of wealth, enough to rival that of the ton."

"I see. So has the man been caught?" I mentally thanked my brother for his question, holding my breath as I waited for Mr. Devensies' answer.

"The Bow Street Runners have plans to catch him tonight at another event where Ms. Chapman is set to make an appearance. We have surmised that she is his intended target, so we have no doubt he will be in attendance at the Covent Garden Theater as well."

Sweat slicked my palms as I clenched them at my sides. My heart was pounding. They were going to arrest Henry tonight. I tried to keep my composure while my mind raced through every scenario I could imagine. I should warn him, shouldn't I? He did not deserve to get caught.

Mr. Devensies winked. "I am certain you will read all about it in the papers in the morrow." He nodded once more. "Well, I shall not keep you any longer. John, we should catch up before either of us leaves London. You can leave word for me at Steven's Hotel." With a last clap on John's shoulder, the older man ambled off.

"What is the time?" I asked John.

He pulled a watch from his pocket, checking the time. "Nearly three, why?"

"I feel a bit tired; I would like to go home and rest if I am to do anything this evening."

Rose grabbed John's hand "I could use a lie down as well. This pregnancy is wearing me out."

The four of us returned to the carriage; Tom and Estelle were chatting away on the driver's seat.

"Welcome back, sir," Tom said.

"I hope you enjoyed the ice," John said. "If you are ready, could you take us back to the house?"

I spent the entire ride back on pins and needles. Once we were back at the home, I needed to find a way to leave again and warn Henry. I chewed the bottom of my lip. With the light still being out, there was no chance for me to hide and find Henry in secret. I could not go alone. I needed to tell Anne and hope she would help me.

I sighed. Every jostle of the carriage as the wheels encountered bumps and holes in the road felt like the ticking of a clock counting down the minutes until it was too late. Henry would be caught.

"What will happen to the Gentleman Thief if he gets caught?" I asked my brother. Anne was glaring at me from the side, though she kept silent. I tried my best to ignore her stares.

John considered my question thoughtfully. "I suppose, unless he manages to slip away like he did after William's trial, he runs a good chance of being hanged."

"Hanged?" I squeezed my hand so tightly, my knuckles turned white. "But he has never harmed anyone and surely public opinion matters?"

"The words of common folk will not matter in a well-publicized case like his. He has taken a lot of money from people with connections. I wager that the judge will rule in favor of the harshest sentencing."

"Even if the money helped the poor and needy?"

"Even then," John concurred. He gazed at me. "Why are you this interested in the Gentleman Thief?"

"Everything I have read about him in the papers has been fascinating. I admit I do not want to see him caught," I said.

John shrugged. "I suppose I do not agree with the man's methods, but I am aware of the immense wealth disparity between all the King's subjects and do think more should be done to ensure a better life quality for everyone." I nodded; my heart still twisted into a tangled mess.

As soon as Tom pulled into the back courtyard and stopped the carriage, I clambered out of my seat. The others could handle bringing in the sweets. I grabbed Anne's hand and pulled her inside.

"What are you doing?"

"Come with me, please. I need to tell you something in confidence." I dragged her up to my room and sat her down on the edge of my bed.

She lifted her brow. "I do not need to guess what this is about."

My expression pained, I said, "I need to warn him."

"And how do you propose you will do that?"

"Come with me," I pleaded. "We can tip him off so he can flee."

"Beth," Anne sighed. "He is still a criminal."

"He does not deserve to die." My voice raised as I uttered my frustration. "You do not understand, I love him."

"Oh, Beth..."

I shook my head, upset at the pity in Anne's voice. "What if it was Willa? What then?"

Anne's eyes darted back and forth. "I..."

I grabbed her hands. "Please, at least let me try."

"What about your family? Will they not think it strange that we left?"

"If we sneak out through the back, we could hail a hackney cab a block away. If all goes well, we could return before anyone has missed us. We said we were going to rest before supper anyway."

Anne avoided my gaze and frowned. "I suppose that could work."

"I am sure it will. We warn Henry and return home post haste."

<h1 style="text-align:center">2 2</h1>

To The Docks

Anne and I waited a half hour, hoping that by then John and Rose would have retired to their room. Downstairs, the front rooms were empty, but we could hear the servants' voices coming from the kitchen and hallway. I looked to Anne. The back exit was out of the question.

She tipped her head to the front entrance. "No one is watching us here. We should leave through the front door."

I glanced around before grasping the handle and turning it gently. The door waved open, and we both exited and closed the door swiftly behind us.

Anne looked up at the windows. "Now off to find a cab."

We strode as fast as our legs would carry us down the pavement. Carriages and single riders traveled up and down the street. A familiar black carriage appeared in the distance, and I held out my arm, waving at the driver.

The man ordered his horse to stop, slowing it down until it halted in front of us.

"Where to, miss?"

"The docks," I said, riffling through my reticule and thrusting coin into his outstretched hand. With a tip of his hat, he jumped down and opened the carriage door for us. We shuffled in and waited for the journey to continue.

The driver dropped us off at the entrance to the docks. I thanked him and, linking arms with Anne, strutted towards the familiar scene. Just last night I had stood here watching the warehouse.

"Where to now?" Anne asked.

"Not far. Perhaps a fifteen-minute walk along the Thames."

The docks were teeming with life; crewmen, shipbuilders, and day laborers, moving cargo from barges and ships to dedicated facilities. We passed by the warehouses, large parcels and crates being lugged into storage, anything that might be needed in the British Empire. Sections of the docks and warehouses were dedicated to specific needs like rubber, textiles, spices, grains, and more. Beyond the docks were plenty of other thriving businesses; laundresses, pubs, brothels, and inns like the one Henry was staying at. I shuddered; it truly was a miracle I had not been spotted. If another man had seen me, he might have mistaken me for one of the birds of paradise.

Anne clung to my side. "We should hurry. I do not like this area." I agreed. Glancing around, I picked up my pace, heading for the inn.

The building looked even shabbier during the day. The "to let" sign was fading and the paint on the wooden sides of the inn was flaking off, revealing dry-rotted wood. The stink from the Thames permeated every inch of the area.

I rushed to the staircase, climbing to the second floor.

"Henry," I yelled, knocking on the door. I waited, listening for footsteps, but beyond the hustle and bustle of other people nearby, I could detect no movement. I knocked again. "Henry, are you there?"

"I do not think he is here," Anne said.

"What's this ruckus all about then?" A broad woman threw open the door to the room beneath us.

Anne glanced up at me, hesitating.

I climbed down the stairs. "We are looking for the man who has been staying here."

Crossing her arms and wiggling her eyebrows at me, the woman said, "And what's it to you?"

"He is my...friend."

"Mmm." Her eyes flashed to my belly. "Knocked you up, has he? Tasted your wares?"

I stepped back, my spine hitting the railing. "No."

"That's what they all say." The woman tutted. "If you want my opinion, I would go back home. I know your lot." She motioned her head at Anne and myself. "Fancy little rich girls looking for their taste of the forbidden fruit. Probably heard a whole lot of sweet talkin' in your ears from that man until you were ripe enough to pluck." She uttered a raspy, lascivious laugh. "Hurry on home before all there is left for you is to join the light skirts a street over."

Anne stepped down and grabbed my hand, glaring at the woman. "Let us leave, she," Anne raked her eyes over the woman's frame, "has no idea what she is talking about."

"You think on it, sweetheart." The woman grinned, revealing a mouth full of blackened, rotten teeth.

"No, thanks," I said, following Anne down the steps. We hurried away from the inn to find another cab.

"What am I supposed to do now?" I asked Anne. "He is not here, but I still have to warn him. If I do not find him, he will be heading straight into a trap."

"You have no idea where he might be?"

I shook my head, a deep V forming between my brows.

Anne pursed her lips. "If you are true about wanting to warn him, there might be no other option than to tell your brother and Rose. We have to hurry as it stands before we are too late to help anyone. I could send a note to Willa as well. At the very least, she might lend us a hand."

A few streets over, Anne and I caught another cab. Sitting inside the compartment, I could not stop my legs from tapping as I fretfully glanced out the window.

"We will never reach him in time," I said with worry. "How are we even supposed to find him at the Covent Garden Theater? The place will be packed."

"You do not know that. We can at least try." Anne did her best to sound reassuring, even going so far as to pat my leg.

Once the driver stopped at our street, Anne confronted the driver.

"Can you deliver a message for me?"

The man scratched his stubble. "I don't have time for messages; I need customers."

She pulled out her reticule. "I will pay you all the money I have on me." Anne pulled out some coin and held it up to the man. "Please."

The driver glanced at the money and huffed. "That is not enough to cover what potential clients could pay. I am running a business not a charity."

I added the money from my bag. "This should more than cover your days' wages."

The man weighed the coins in his hands, his lips lifting into a crooked smile. "Pleasure doing business with you ladies. Now, what's the message and where's it going?"

Anne straightened and enunciated clearly. "Go to the Marquis of Bambreich's house and ask for Willa Balfour. Tell her that we need her help with the duke and to meet us as soon as she can either at Beth's or, if it is late, at the Covent Garden Theater."

The driver repeated Anne's words. Anne nodded, pleased.

"Who should I say the message is from?"

"Anne Blakeley."

With that sorted, Anne and I needed to speak to my brother and Rose. My stomach cramped at the thought, but I had no other choice; I needed to save Henry if I could.

I crossed the pavement and walked up the few short steps to the front door and knocked.

"Miss Easton?" Bartley, the butler seemed puzzled at our appearance. "I thought you and Ms. Blakeley had retired upstairs."

"Who is that?" John's voice sounded from the sitting room.

"Your sister and Ms. Blakeley, sir." Bartley raised his voice to be heard.

"My sister?" John turned into the hallway, his eyes widening when he spotted Anne and me standing in the doorway. "What are the both of you doing out there?"

I stepped inside. "John, I need to speak with you and Rose, this instant."

John frowned and looked to Anne who said nothing. "Alright, Rose is in the sitting room; we can speak there. What is this all about?"

"Do you remember that man from earlier—"

"Devensies? What does he have to do with anything?"

I hesitated, not knowing how I should broach the subject. "He—Devensies, I mean—spoke about the Gentleman Thief. I know him."

"What do you mean?"

"We should get to Rose first," I suggested, nervous about John's darkening expression.

"Fine, but you need to tell me everything." He entered the sitting room where Rose sat on the settee, her legs folded beneath her, lazily swirling a spoon in a cup of tea on the stand beside her. She had a book propped open on her lap.

Rose smiled up at us and was about to say hello when she spotted John's expression. She tilted her head towards him. "What's going on?"

John rubbed his brow. "Ask my sister. I found her and Anne at our doorstep talking about the Gentleman Thief or Harry Doyle or whatever his alias is."

"His name is Henry," I corrected.

My brother snorted and Rose's eyes flashed back to me, her brows raised, waiting for an explanation.

I stared at my feet, rubbing my elbow. "Anne and I left the house to warn the Gentleman Thief." My voice came out uncertain and soft. But the ticking of the grandfather clock reminded me that time was of the essence. I closed my eyes, cleared my throat, and started anew. My eyes connected with my brother's and I straightened, shaking off my nerves.

"Henry—the Gentleman Thief—has been courting me these past weeks. I will not let him get arrested."

John froze and glared while Rose rubbed her chin.

"I thought you had been seeing a duke?"

Face turning red, John turned to Rose. "A duke? You knew Beth had been seeing someone?"

Next to me, Anne shuffled backwards as if to distance herself from us. I could not say that I blamed her.

"Wait, John. It is my fault. I asked Rose to keep my confidence. If you want to blame anyone, blame me."

John let out a dry laugh. "Oh, I am. Now, were you courted by a duke or the Gentleman Thief or both." He tapped his foot against the hardwood floors.

"The Gentleman Thief is the duke. I pretended to be Willa when she did not want to meet the duke, but the duke was actually the Gentleman Thief."

"Why warn him?" John's words simmered.

"I love him," I said it as plainly as I could. John seemed as if he was choking on his own saliva.

"Love? While the man was pretending to be a duke?" He shook his head. "Do not be ridiculous, Beth." John's eyes narrowed, glancing at me. "Did he make any untoward advances?"

"John, stop. I am old enough to know what I am doing. I do not need your protection for everything." I raised my voice, glaring at my brother. "I said I loved him, and I meant it. I do not know whether Henry feels the same, but I cannot let him get arrested and be hanged." I raised my hands, pleading.

"I implore you, help me warn him before it is too late. He is a good man. If you love me, I need you to support me."

John's gaze turned distant, his shoulders, which had been rigid, sagged.

His down-turned face tugged at my heartstrings; a heaviness filled my chest. "I know you mean the best for me," I said, softening my voice. "But I am a grown woman. I need to make my own decisions."

A watery smile tugged at my brother's lips. "I know. I am so proud of you, Beth, but I worry about you. You were all I had after our parents..." He swallowed. "You were still so young, and I had to be the head of the house, make sure you were happy and thriving. That is all I ever wanted for you."

My vision blurred as tears welled up in my eyes. I crossed the distance and enveloped my brother in a hug, sniffling against his shirt. "You are not alone," I muttered. "You will always have me and Rose. And do not forget the staff; Mrs. Avery would smack you with a spoon if she could hear you. And your tenants love you. So many people count on you and admire you."

John's grip tightened. "I am sorry for being such an overbearing brother."

"All the best are," I reminded John. He chuckled, exhaling deeply.

"What about this gentleman thief then?" Rose said from the settee.

John released me and rolled his eyes, smiling a bit. "I suppose we will help."

"Good," I said, letting out a breath.

Feeling safe to step forward again, Anne said, "I have

sent a note to Willa. If it arrives in time, she might be able to help."

I nodded. "We will have to go to the Covent Garden Theater and try to find Henry before the Bow Street Runners do."

"How will we recognize him?" Rose pursed her lips and uncurled from the settee.

"I have seen him before," John said, rubbing the back of his neck. "It has been a while, but I should still be able to recognize him."

"He is tall, dark, and Irish," I added.

John shook his head and raised his brows in part wonder and disbelief. "I suppose we should ready ourselves for a night at the theater."

23

❦

Covent Garden Theater

Coiffed and dressed in an appropriate evening gown, I mingled with the crowd gathering on the sidewalk outside the Covent Garden theater, its grand facade and gated alcoves one of the main draws of the popular market square. Four grand white columns obscured the view to the entrance where John stood beneath the covered walkway, purchasing tickets.

"Have you seen Willa?" I looked to Anne, who fidgeted with her jacket.

She shook her head, eyes darting back and forth. "No, have you seen—"

"No." I wondered whether Willa had received Anne's message and if she would arrive on time to help. If she did, perhaps Melinda would be with her as well. The bookshop owner was never far from the marquis' side these days.

I scanned the crowd for a tall man with dark curly hair, soulful brown eyes, and a mouth that held a perpetual smirk—a face I had come to adore. But it remained absent in the crowd outside. I kept looking, studying each face until my breath hitched. I spotted one of the Bow Street Runners. The man stood half-hidden near the side of the building, recognizable by his familiar uniform of black buttoned-down jacket and tan trousers. If there was one, there had to be more; Devensies did say they were planning on arresting him this evening. Besides the men in uniform, there most likely were also constables in plain clothing circulating the theater.

"John needs to hurry," I whispered to Anne. "If we do not find Henry and warn him right now the Bow Street Runners are going to find him. They are already here."

"They are?" Anne's eyes widened. I discreetly pointed out the constable I had identified before. A small frown appeared between Anne's brow. "As soon as we can enter the theater we will have to split up as to cover more ground."

I nodded, taking note again of my brother. He and Rose seemed to have finished purchasing the tickets. They were walking towards us with grim and determined faces, contrasting heavily with the other cheerful and excited people who were looking forward to watching an opera.

"Ready?" I asked Anne before pushing my way through the crowd to reach my brother faster. Anne followed in my footsteps.

Once I reached him and Rose, John held out the paper slips. "I have the tickets."

"Thank you." My brows knitted together. "I hope we can find Henry in time." I clutched the ticket to my chest. "We should split up and head in different directions once we are inside."

I gathered my heavy skirts in my left hand to give my legs more room to move while John nodded. "Let us meet at our home after if we can or send a note if you are prohibited from doing so." He pursed his lips and sighed, a small twitch of his brows showing his concern. "Be careful, please."

"I will." I strode towards the entrance, brushing past people mingling and socializing outside and veered around one of the columns. A valet was checking tickets and sliding back a velvet rope to let guests through.

My palms were sweating, but I flashed him my ticket, forcing my features into a mask of pleasantness. The man checked my ticket before tipping his hat and creating an opening for me to pass through.

The grand foyer opened up before me. Straight ahead there was the entrance to the pit while to the right and left hallways with walls the color of egg yolks were lined with built-in benches. Pedestals topped with Grecian statues raising their arms to the skies interspersed the seats. The entire space was warmed pleasantly by stoves. A double staircase led to three rows of private box seats.

I avoided one of the ladies carrying around a tray of fruits and bee-lined for the pits. The stage was still curtained, but many men and women had already taken their seats. Candlelight from wall sconces and an ornate multi-tiered chandelier hanging from the ceiling illuminated the entire horseshoe-shaped theater. Despite the lighting, there were too many faces for me to recognize Henry easily. I wrung my hands and walked down the first aisle on the left. I glanced up at the private boxes, but from this angle, I could not recognize anyone, even if it had been my own brother. Only the pale green wainscoting on the outside of the boxes was visible. If Henry was not in the pits, I would have to search each box.

I kept moving down the rows, searching for a dark-haired man.

Third row.

My heart skipped a beat, and I moved forward, placing my hand on his shoulder.

"Henry."

Green eyes looked back at me. "Can I help you?"

It was not him. I snatched my hand back as if a snake had bitten me. "I apologize, I thought you were someone else."

The man laughed and returned to his conversation with a companion.

I wanted to close my eyes and yell Henry's name, but I could not alert the Bow Street Runners. Who knew which person here was one of them, merely waiting until they spotted Henry? No, I had to keep going. I had to find Henry before it was too late.

Hiking up my skirts once more, I hurried down the aisles, my head flicking left and right, looking for Henry's face but finding none that matched his.

Right. If he was not in the pits then he was in a private box at one of three upper circles. *Or he is not here at all*, the back of my mind whispered. Perhaps he had been tipped off or Devensies had been wrong. I braced myself against the wall near the exit. I could not count on that. I turned out of the pits to look up at John and Rose. They halted.

"You did not find him?"

I shook my head.

"The private boxes then? We shall go right."

I flashed my brother and Rose a pained smile before hurrying to the double staircase and rushing up the steps as fast I could. I worried about the attention I was drawing as my breathing turned ragged. Perhaps I should join Rose on more hikes when we returned to Hawthorne.

I wondered briefly where Anne was, but I had no time to contemplate the matter further. She would turn up and there were more important matters right now.

By my own fast deduction, I figured I would start my search at the top circle and work my way down, peeking behind each curtain to look for Henry. I did not find him at the top circle and neither at the second. My heart beating in my chest, I reached the final circle of private boxes.

"Good heavens."

I pulled open the first curtain to reveal two women, a mother and daughter, judging by their ages, clutching their fans to their chests, and a middle-aged man who scowled at me.

"What is this intrusion about?"

"Wrong box." I stepped back and dropped the velvet cloth. From afar, I became aware of the swell of music; the stage curtains must have opened. Thundering applause roared through the theater as people clapped for the start of the opera.

Hoping I would be fortuitous this time, I darted into the next box.

"Beth?" Henry turned away from the stage and stood, mouth agape. "What are you doing here?"

My eyes honed in on him and I stopped. My words momentarily frozen on my lips. It was not until Mary Chapman spoke that I reacted.

"Edmund, who is this?" she said, fluttering her lashes and stepping closer to Henry who in turn seemed lost for words. "Tell her to leave."

I ignored her. "The Bow Street Runners are here," I said, eyes focused on the man in front of me.

Realization dawned on his face. He looked down at Mary and then back at me. "We need to leave."

Mary grabbed Henry's arm. "Go where? With her?" She huffed and pouted. "I thought we were going to watch the opera."

Henry pulled his arm from her grasp. "Please, continue watching the opera without me. I am leaving."

"What?" Mary glared.

Henry turned to me. "Ready?"

"Yes," I lowered my voice. "But we need to be careful. I have spotted one Bow Street Runner outside the theater so they most likely have the building surrounded."

Henry nodded, frowning. "I cannot believe you came to warn me."

"It is best not to get into it now, but if you had been at the room you were renting, I could have warned you a whole lot sooner."

Henry's brow twitched, his eyes briefly sparkling before turning serious. "I believe you." He lifted the heavy draped curtain.

Mary raised her voice. "This is outrageous. My father will hear about this. Your behavior is nothing like that of a gentleman. Walking off with your harlot," she spat at me.

"This has nothing to do with you. Goodbye, Mary," he said with barely a glance at her.

His hand enveloped mine, his warmth doing much to settle my nerves. Henry ducked underneath the curtain into the hallway, taking me with him.

Standing in the dusky hallway, his eyes pierced mine. "Do you think we can leave through the front?"

I considered his question. There had been a lot of people at the entrance; if we managed to reach it, we could disappear into the crowd, but only if they were still there. "Perhaps."

I chewed my lip, wanting to ask if he had other ideas, but he spoke first, his eyes flashing to something behind me.

"Too late."

His nose flared as his hand gripped my hand tighter.

"I see him!" a voice yelled behind me.

Mary followed us out of the private box, about to argue some more, but Henry returned his gaze to me.

"We need to run."

Henry pulled me in the opposite direction, my legs tangling in my skirts. With my free hand, I pulled them up so I could run, not caring that I was flashing bared legs at the two Bow Street Runners behind us. I hoped it would distract them.

"Where to?"

Henry's eyes raced to and fro. We could not keep going; the hallway ended in nothing but a wall.

"Trust me," he said, his dark eyes imploring me. I nodded. We burst headfirst into another box, disturbing a portly fellow and his mistress.

The woman shrieked and fanned herself. Henry grabbed my waist and lifted up me over the wainscoting to much shouting from the gray-haired portly fellow.

The drop to the pit being only a few feet, I made it to

the ground without difficulties. All around me, guests were gasping, whispering, and pointing.

"Apologies," I mumbled, turning my head towards Henry.

The portly man clawed at Henry's jacket, trying to hold him there, veins throbbing at his temple.

Henry reached his arm back and hit the man square in the jaw. The man's grip loosened, and Henry pulled away, jumping over the front of the private box. Henry's feet thudded the ground next to me, and he snatched my hand once more.

"Follow them!" the Bow Street Runners yelled from the box. The portly man added to the noise by screaming, "He hit me! Stop that man."

I glanced back while running along the aisle to see the two men climbing out of the same box, red faced. I nearly tripped and returned my gaze forward.

The stage was filled with dancers performing a number for the first act, a soprano belting her notes at the center. However, most of the attendees in the pits were now paying attention to our flight and the two bumbling Bow Street Runners faltering behind us. The chatter was deafening.

"We need to get to the back of the theater," Henry said from my side as we reached the stage.

Grabbing my waist, Henry lifted me onto the wooden stage. As soon as my knees hit the boards, I scrambled forward and held out my hand to pull him up.

My eyes locked with my brother standing in the pits. He gave me a quick hurried wave before he and Rose rushed into the Bow Street Runners chasing us. They worked hard, distracting our pursuers and blocking the aisle while Henry and I got back to standing.

Music screeched to a halt.

We rushed past the group of dancers on stage, the soprano glaring at us as we stole her spot light. Henry and I veered off to the back.

"They won't be long," I rushed out. "Is there an exit somewhere?"

Behind the stage, the theater looked like a maze of wooden beams and ropes. Men manned pulley systems to lift curtains and move props on stage. Their attention was on us as we passed them by. I was grateful no one had tried to stop us.

"Down the hall to the left." A young boy shrugged from a corner.

"Thank you."

I could hear footsteps speeding up behind us. Henry and I ran past previous set designs and racks of costumes, making sure our feet would not tangle in unused twine and props. We hurried past green rooms and dressing rooms until we bumped into the exit.

A darkening sky welcomed us as Henry opened the door. A soft breeze cooled my flushed face.

"Got ye."

I jerked. A meaty hand grabbed my shoulder and on the opposite side of me, another Bow Street Runner pulled Henry into a vice. He struggled against his captor.

"Thought you could outrun us, eh?" The man that held me licked his lips as he stared at Henry. "Naw. That there bounty on your head is enough to have this whole place cornered." His fingers dug into my skin.

"Let me go."

I flinched as the man laughed loudly beside my ear. His

putrid breath clogging my nose. "And what've we got here." He motioned at Henry before gripping me tighter. "His accomplice or his light skirt?"

"Take your hands off of her." Henry's melodic voice deepened to something of a growl.

"Or what?" the constable holding me said. "Seems to me you don't have much of a say."

The other constable grabbed rope from his pocket, roughly pulled Henry's arms behind his back, and tied them firmly together. "We'll be taking the both of you to the Home Office." He shoved Henry forward.

The man holding me glanced around the pavement, distracted for a moment. His beady eyes fixed on his partner. "You got them? I should tell the others the search is finished."

The constable lifted his head. "Yeah, just let me tie her up too. Don't want her thinking she could run."

The Bow Runner pushed me towards his partner. My feet slipped, and I stumbled into Henry.

"She has nothing to do with this. It is me that you are after." Henry gritted his teeth. "The girl does not even know who I am."

"Is that so?" The constable smirked. "Then why was she calling you Henry?" He lifted his hand and pushed Henry's head forward. "Thought you was going by Edmund, havin' a little turn at playing a duke."

Henry seethed as the man tied my hand to his.

"My brother will find us," I whispered to Henry while the constable pulled the knot tight enough for the fibers to burn my skin. I hissed at the sharp pain.

The constable straightened and checked the road. "I'll put

them on a cab. Graves, you go warn the others, and I'll meet you at the office."

Perhaps sixty feet away there were a couple of Hackney cabs parked and waiting for customers. My eyes met Henry's; my brows scrunched up in worry. What were we supposed to do now? His fingers untangled and reached for the hand that was tied to his. Thumb skimming the outside of my palm, he mouthed one word.

Wait.

His eyes implored me to listen. I nodded, determined to follow his lead. There was no other option.

The other Bow Street Runner ambled away, returning back into the bowels of the theater. Short notes of music drifted out as the back door opened and closed.

"Walk," the remaining constable said without feeling. When I did not react fast enough, he pushed me into the street. His grip tight, we loped around a passing carriage. "I should thank you for returning to London." The constable sneered behind us. "With you finally caught, we'll receive a large sum of money. Much better prospect than any sole thief finder nabbing you in the countryside." He punctuated his words with another shove.

Henry stifled a groan. I could tell the rope was digging into his skin, but he remained stoic. "I would have rather stayed in the country, fresher air and all."

The constable snorted. "Get your last words out now. Before long, you'll be sitting in a jail cell. Where do you think you are going next, hmmm? I bet your little light skirt here knows."

The Bow Street Runner was ogling me with an evil grin. I turned my chin, refusing to look at him.

"No? I'll answer for you then. That one's a piece of gallows bait." He pressed us onto the sidewalk across the street. A group of men walked in our direction.

Henry stopped and threw his head back, hitting the constable square in the nose.

"Now. Run."

The constable's grip on the rope loosened as he lifted his hand to clutch his nose.

"Bugger." Blood spurted down his chin.

Henry pulled me along, ripping the rest of the rope from the constable's hands.

"Now's our chance."

With his hands still tied behind his back and my right fastened to his, we ran. Feet pounding down the pavement, we pushed past the men.

"Stop them!" the Bow Street Runner gurgled.

"Do not look back." Henry kept running, urging me forward.

One of the bystanders grabbed for my sleeve, but I shrugged him off. I could not stop. My wrist ached and my heart thudded at the back of my throat. We needed to get away and hide. The first turn, we veered left into a back alley.

"Is he still coming?" My breathing had gone ragged and my stomach turned, ready to spill its contents.

"I do not think he will let us go that easily." Henry's face whipped back and forth, looking for the next route. Brick walls loomed on either side of us. We swerved around broken crates left in our path.

"Doors." He lifted his chin towards the alley exits.

We rushed towards the first entrance. I pulled the handle, but it was locked.

There was a shrill whistle and a man yelling, "Where'd they go?"

I grabbed at the next handle and was luckier. The handle turned and the door creaked open. Henry and I burst into the back of a kitchen, kicking over a stack of pots.

"Apologies," I shouted as we maneuvered past the cook and scullery maids manning the stoves.

Sweat dribbled down my spine. The front of the eatery was packed with couples and men dining and conversing.

"We have to keep going," Henry urged.

A barrel-chested man sidled from behind the counter and stepped in our way. "What is the meaning of this?"

"Move." Henry shoved past him. The man teetered on his legs and stumbled into a table, toppling the contents onto the diners.

I gaped at the sight, but Henry did not stop to look. He pulled me with him as he pushed against the main entrance.

We had reached the main Covent Garden Square. Unfortunately, since the sun had started to dip, the place was no longer filled with throngs of people. Only a handful of men were traversing the cobblestones at this time of day. We would not be able to hide in a crowd.

Henry was pulling me to the right when I spotted a short woman with a big head of brown curls in the distance. She waved at me.

Melinda.

"Henry, follow me."

His eyes seemed wary though he made no objection as we ran straight across the square. Shouts and whistles behind us turned louder. My legs ached, but I pushed through the burning in my calves.

Breathing hard, I yelled for Melinda. "Do you have a way out?"

The bookshop owner pulled out a pendant from beneath her dress' bust-line. "Grab my hand."

"What?" Henry frowned, an incredulous expression on his face.

The same constable shouted, "Stop," though more men had joined him in his pursuit and were also raising their voices, filling the ever-darkening sky with the sounds of feet slapping against stone and the angry tones of men.

"Do what she says."

I bumped against Henry, turning to face our pursuers so Melinda could take a hold of our hands.

Nearing fast, a toothy grin covered the Bow Street Runner's face. He reached out his hand as he ran towards us.

"Got ye," he said as I felt Melinda's hand touch mine and everything turned black.

2 4

The Magical Bookshop

My back hit the floor with a thud and my tied-up hand crushed beneath my and Henry's combined weight. Hissing, I rolled to my side while Henry blinked, dazed from the impact, my hand still pinned beneath me. He groaned and after a bit of fumbling managed to sit up.

Henry motioned his head down, gesturing towards his lower body.

"My left pocket."

With what little slack I had, I scrambled onto my knees and dug my free hand into his pocket. My fingers curled around a cool, oblong shaped item. I pulled it out to see that it was a pocketknife, its shaft a pretty amber and brown tortoise shell.

I did not need Henry to spell out what I needed to do.

One handed, I lifted the folded knife up to my face and pried it open using my teeth.

230

"Where in the world are we?" Henry muttered.

"You are in my bookshop," Melinda answered as I cut through a piece of rope. "The both of you found yourself in quite a situation."

Henry's bindings fell away, and he gingerly rubbed his wrists, angry red marks marring his tanned skin. With the tension on the rope gone, I managed to cut away the twine around my wrist as well. My wrist throbbed and ached.

Henry stood and turned around to gaze at his surroundings, gaping at the rows of bookshelves and books. "How did we get here?" His brows puckered as he looked questioningly at Melinda.

Melinda spread her arms, swiveling from side to side. "You are currently standing inside my magical bookshop."

I swallowed, pressing my palm against my chest, hoping my breathing would even out. "Did we move through time? Is this what happened to Rose and William?"

Melinda smiled and shook her head. "No, this time we have merely moved through space. This place functions a bit like a holding area. At this moment, we are not really anywhere but at the same time we are everywhere."

Henry bent towards me and helped me off the ground while keeping a suspicious eye on Melinda. "What is this talk about moving through time and space?"

Holding on to his arms, I steadied myself. I chewed my lip. Henry must be overwhelmed with the new information bombarding him. When Rose first told me, I had been too baffled to respond at all. Now, while knowing time-travel was real, I was still shocked to see the magic for myself. "Melinda is a time-traveler." I paused to gauge Henry's reaction.

"Time-traveler...? How do you —" He stopped, shaking his head.

"My brother's wife is from the future. She showed up at our estate and fell in love with John; that is how I also met Melinda. There is more which I can tell you later if you'd like."

Henry's eyes narrowed. "Will we be able to return home? Are we stuck here?" He let go of my body and paced the floor.

Melinda walked to a wooden register topped with a device that looked like a cash register though it hardly resembled any that I had seen before. She turned around the corner, bending and disappearing from view before she popped back up holding two clear bottles in her hands.

"Some water," she said, thrusting them towards Henry and myself.

I examined the strange material that crinkled in my hand as I pressed it.

"You twist the cap." Melinda pointed at the blue lid.

I did as she said and opened the bottle. Sticking out my tongue, I carefully tasted the clear liquid. It was indeed water. Grateful for something to drink, I threw back the bottle, cool water soothing my parched throat. My lungs still strained to catch up as my body returned to resting. I swiped my forehead.

Observing me, Henry soon followed suit, draining his bottle.

"Thank you," I told Melinda. My eyes flitted to the ceiling; a strange light lit up the inside of the shop.

"That is electricity."

The words were new, and I decided to inspect the shop,

walking past the shelves, my fingers trailing the spines of books.

"Beth, Henry," Melinda addressed us. Henry pushed back the book he was holding and turned his attention to the book shop owner. "Take your time to catch your breath. I will let your family know that you are safe for now. Be back in in a bit." She pulled out the same pendant and disappeared in front of our eyes.

Henry dropped the empty water bottle. "Is that what happened to us?"

I nodded.

Henry scratched his head. "This is a lot to wrap my head around. I do not know what to say." He exhaled, dropping his arms to his side.

Now that it was just the two of us, it hit me that we had made it. We had escaped the Bow Street Runners. Henry was safe.

My chest deflated and I sprinted towards him, throwing my arms around his waist. "I thought they caught us, that we were going to prison." I pressed my head against his chest.

"You were so brave." Henry caressed my hair and rested his chin against my temple. His arms tightened around me, warming my skin. "Brave but foolish."

I pulled back to gaze into his brown eyes. "I could not let them take you."

"Despite pushing you away?" Henry's eyes darkened.

"Despite everything." My chest heaved. "I was so worried when I found out the Bow Street Runners were after you."

Henry lowered his head and kissed my temple. He let go

of my arms to cup my face. "I cannot explain how grateful I am that you came for me." He pressed his forehead against mine. "From the moment I saw you at that ball I could not stop thinking about you. You plagued my every thought and dream. Guilt for deceiving you gnawed at me very core every moment we spent together. I wanted to confess the truth and beg you to take me as I am while I was under the assumption you were Willa. I do not care that you lied about your identity; I did the same." My heart leaped at his words. Henry's breath heated my cheek. "Can you forgive me for lying?"

"Yes."

Henry crushed his lips against mine, my body molding itself to his. The adrenaline still coursing through my veins urged me on. I raked my hand through his soft, curly hair.

Henry nipped at my lips. "Will you run away with me?" he asked in a deep, hungry tone. My skin tingled and I kissed him, breathless. His question seemed to echo a similar question I was once asked by Mr. Danby. Then, running away had been a terrible mistake, but this time my mind was clear. Running away with Henry could never be a mistake. I was his equal, and I loved him.

"I will go anywhere with you."

Henry placed a tender kiss upon my lips. "I do not have much to offer you, but everything I have is yours, if you will have me."

I smiled tenderly. "Everything you have will be enough. However, we cannot stay in London."

Henry grabbed my hand and caressed the rope burns on my wrist; he fluttered a soft kiss against my skin. "We shall leave for Ireland. I suppose I should introduce you to my brother, the real Duke of Cashel."

"The real duke?" I stepped back. "I thought you were impersonating a stranger. Why would you do this if you were the brother of a duke? How does no one know?"

Henry glanced off to the side, shoulders rising as he breathed in before launching into his explanation. "Edmund is my half-brother. My mother was a scullery maid working at the castle when our father seduced her and got her with child. He turned her out and refused to acknowledge me. Edmund was still young but aware enough to realize we were related. Of course, gossip spread in the town as well. My mother was treated as a pariah and lived hand to mouth while caring for me until she passed."

Henry's gaze turned inward, his expression pained as he recalled his past.

"What was her name?" I took his hand in mine.

"Moira." A wistful smile appeared on his face. "She is why I do all of this. The previous duke threw my mother away like she was garbage, and she is not the only person discarded by society. I want to give us regular folk a voice and a chance to thrive. Why should these predatory noblemen hold all the power?"

"That is a commendable objective."

"My brother sent out solicitors to find me once our father passed away. While I have not been officially acknowledged, he has given me a family and a place to live. He is a good man and has taken it upon himself to change the lives of his tenants for the better."

"I would love to meet him."

Henry's eyes darted around the room. "As long as we can leave this...shop."

"Melinda will return, and we will leave." My eyes drifted to a nook in a corner of the shop, outfitted with a padded bench. "Let us take a seat and wait." I sidled up with Henry and rested my head on his shoulder. He drew slow circles on my arm with his finger, murmuring sweet words against my ear. "Henry..."

"Mmm?" his voice reverberated against me.

"Will we be able to visit my family once this is all over?"

"Not immediately, no. The Bow Street Runners do not know my true identity, but it is better to be safe and lay low for a while. Though, your family could visit Ireland."

I cleared my throat. "That is a relief. I think you would like my brother and his wife. John has a good report with his tenants, and Rose even runs a school for the children. Perhaps, once we can return, I could show you Hawthorne."

"I would love to see your home." Henry lifted my chin and kissed me. "I wish we had—"

"What?" I angled my face more towards him, eager for him to finish his sentence.

His lips skimmed mine, yearning in his eyes. "I wish I could kiss you into a stupor until your lips are swollen a bright red and you would beg me to touch you. I want to gaze at your body and revel in your beauty." He pulled me into his lap, his eyes flitting to my injured wrist.

Heat from his chest radiated against my back. My cheeks burned and my pulse raced.

"But you are hurt, and we are in a strange place with no idea when that woman will return."

I arched my back, leaning in to Henry and running my palm up his chest. My fingers arched around the edges of his shirt, touching his silky skin and playing with the dark hairs growing there.

Henry closed his eyes and groaned. "Beth, you are testing my patience."

His obvious distress sent shivers down my spine. I wanted this man more than anything. My body ached for his touch.

He ran his hand through my blonde hair. "You cannot imagine how badly I want you, mo ghrá, but we have a long journey ahead of us, and I want to do this right. I need to do this right."

I trailed my finger lower down his chest. "As long as it is with you, it will be right."

Henry's eyes drifted across the front of my body until he gazed deeply into my eyes. I darted forward, tasting his lips. He deepened our kiss, tongue exploring my mouth while I turned to liquid against him.

The floorboards creaked, and I broke our kiss.

Clearing her throat, Melinda stepped into view. My face flushed as I untangled myself from Henry, heat still running through my limbs. Henry composed himself beside me, straightening his shirt.

She quirked her brow, flashing me a knowing smile. "Are you both ready to return?"

I nodded.

"Let us not dawdle then." She took a hold of her pendant.

This time I took my time to stare at the emerald stone that was cradled inside a cage of fine metalwork. The stone emitted a faint glow as Melinda gripped it in her left hand. Henry and I reached for her other hand.

25

Farewell

"Beth." John strode towards me. "Are you alright?"

I nodded, disoriented from the sudden shift in location, my vision still focusing on my new surroundings. Though the sky was dark, cloaking the world in shadows, I recognized that we stood in the enclosed back garden of our rented London town home. Their faces lit by a lantern, Tom and Estelle peeked from the stables together with Anne and Willa.

Once John ascertained my safety, he turned his attention to Henry, scowling. "What is the meaning of involving my sister in your dangerous schemes?" He shoved his hand against Henry's chest. "You are incredibly fortunate you managed to escape. If it had not been for Beth's pleading, we would not have troubled ourselves with your affairs."

Henry lowered his gaze, remaining placid despite John's shoving.

I pushed John's arm away. "Stop it."

John shook his head. "You could have been arrested alongside that man. I think you have done enough for now. You saved the Gentleman Thief and can return home while he," John glared at Henry, "will be leaving for Ireland this moment." He lifted his hand and motioned Tom forward. "Ready the carriage."

"John Easton," I thundered, snapping his gaze back to me. "I will not leave Henry. If we leave, we leave together."

I grabbed Henry's hand and stepped beside him, keeping my eyes firmly pointed at John. "I will always be your sister, but I am old enough to make my own decisions. You listened to me earlier today so please do so again. I love the man beside me."

My eyes flitted to Rose who flashed me an encouraging smile. "And I am of a mind to stay with him forever. In fact," I turned to Henry, a shy smile creeping up my face. "I know this is not traditional, but would you do me the honor of becoming my husband?"

Henry's eyes crinkled and he squeezed my hand.

"Beth," John protested.

"This has nothing to do with you," I told John.

"I am still your brother."

I shot him a steely glare. "Then support my decision."

Rose pulled my brother's shoulder. "John, let her choose what is right. If they love each other, isn't that the most important?"

A multitude of expressions flashed across his face. His voice softened. "If you go, I will no longer be able to protect you."

"I no longer need your protection; I need your support."

John stepped back and remained silent as I turned my face to look up at Henry. "So, will you? Marry me, that is?"

Henry's face widened into a grin, and he pulled me in, lifting me up by my waist. "Yes." His Irish lilt danced against my ear as he buried his chin against my shoulder before returning me to the ground.

Trying to suppress his smile, he nodded at John, though his expression turned serious and sincere. "I will protect Beth with my body and my life if need be. As long as I am here no harm will come to her, that I promise."

This time, Rose spoke. "Will you continue being the Gentleman Thief?"

Henry hesitated. "I want to continue the work I have started, but I will not put Beth in harm's way. Wherever possible, I shall try to continue helping impoverished mothers legitimately."

"Perhaps John can help with that. We could set up a charity of our own, run it where it is needed."

John and Rose had a nonverbal conversation, her brows lifting and receding until John sighed. "It is something to consider. However, there is still the matter of the Bow Street Runners; I doubt they will give up their prey this easily." John tilted his head and pursed his lips, looking at Henry. "There is a handsome sum on your head."

Henry's brows creased. "They might send out men to check the ports if they cannot find me in London. They do not know my true identity, but my accent is difficult to hide."

"I considered the same. The only thing is to ride for Bristol immediately to board a boat to Cork. If you...and Beth," John glanced at my and sighed again, "leave now, you might reach the port before them."

Henry brushed his thumb along his chin. "We could take the carriage up to Liverpool or Holyhead. They might not expect us to take the longer route."

John glanced at the carriage in the stables which had been readied by Tom. He shook his head. "There are too many of them. Most likely they will send out men in every direction; you are too recognizable. No, getting the both of you safely on the nearest boat and on your way to Ireland is the best choice."

My chest tightened as I looked at John, Rose, and Estelle's faces. I realized it could be a long while before I would see them again. My heart clenched at the sight of Anne, her hand clutched tightly by Willa's. I would miss my best friend and I felt sad I would not get to know Willa more but at least they had each other.

John nodded at the stableman. "Tom, take the carriage out front while Beth and Henry ready themselves."

While Tom grabbed the reins of the horse already fastened in front of the carriage, I hugged my brother. "I will miss you."

He kissed my cheek. "We will see each other again, soon."

Next, I hugged Rose who squeezed me tight while John shook Henry's hand.

"Take care of her," John said.

"I promise." Henry nodded gravely. "Why not visit Ireland? You could attend the wedding there."

"Oh, please, John?" I wanted my family present when I said my vows to Henry. "Please say you'll come."

"Once we've settled our affairs at Hawthorne, we will follow you to Ireland." He turned to his Estelle. "While Rose says her goodbyes will you retrieve a suitcase with clothing for Beth?"

My French maid nodded and hurried off into the home.

"I will return in a moment as well." John followed Estelle.

Melinda, who had been standing and gawking during our reunion, walked towards me. She also pulled me into a hug. "Good luck, Beth. This was not what I imagined, but I am happy you have found your happy ever after."

Puzzled at her words, I returned her hug.

She scraped her throat. "Well, I shall leave you all to it. Good luck on your journey."

Melinda vanished, and we were left waiting for John and Estelle to return.

Anne stepped forward, her eyes dark in her ashened face. She enveloped me into a hug, the cold tip of her nose pressing against my earlobe. "Stay safe," she urged, squeezing tighter.

"Visit me in Ireland?"

"I would not dare miss your wedding."

When Anne and I finished saying our farewells, Willa also hugged me. I swallowed down the lump in my throat. Saying goodbye to my friends and family made leaving for Ireland feel very real and sudden. I sighed and smiled wistfully at everyone.

The evening was a blueish-black with moths flurrying past as they moved to surrounding flowers. In the distance, an owl hooted.

"I'll make sure we will be there in time for your wedding." Rose pulled her opera coat tighter around herself. "And you both are always welcome back at Hawthorne once the interest around you," she smirked at Henry, "has died down. I am certain tomorrow's papers will be giving a thorough account of the Gentleman Thief's escape from the Bow Street Runners. It is doubtful that the bounty on your head will ever disappear, but perhaps if you hang up your hat, they might never connect it to you. John can help find you a respectable position."

Henry inclined his head in thanks. "I am much obliged, though I am certain my brother will help with the latter as well."

John returned from the house and pressed bank notes into my hand. "To ensure a safe passing and lodging along the way." The crease between his brow had not lessened, but he smiled as he looked at me. "Good luck." Estelle carried two heavy suitcases.

"Goodbye," I told my family and friends, then Henry and I followed Estelle through the gate. Tom, wearing a hat and long black coat, waited for us in the driver's seat. Henry helped Estelle fasten my two suitcases at the back of the carriage.

I reached for Estelle so I could give her a hug, but my ladies maid shook her head. "Mademoiselle, I am accompanying Tom. We will say our goodbyes at the port. Now hurry." She flashed a determined smile and climbed up beside Tom. He handed her a blanket to cover her legs.

"Ready?" Henry asked.

My eyes turned from Estelle. "Yes."

Tom rode all night, reaching the outskirts of Bristol as the first rays of sunshine warmed the dew-covered fields. I pushed myself up from Henry's lap and stared out the window, bleary-eyed and tired beyond belief. I had not managed to sleep a wink. Henry plucked some stray hairs from my forehead and cheek.

"We will arrive at the port soon. So far, we have been fortuitous. Let us hope our fortunes remain the same until we reach Cork." His lips brushed my cheek. "We will have to keep our heads down until we are well on our way."

Tom steered the carriage as near to the floating docks as he was able. Ships lay docked along the river Avon, only a short boat ride from the ocean. Men scurried to and fro as cargo was hauled and lifted upon decks by way of pulley systems. Ship hands rotated the heavy crates and lowered them to the deck. A horn sounded in the distance.

Henry and I exited the carriage, the scent of salted air heavy as it whipped at my loosened hair. A tapestry of pinks and oranges covered the morning sky.

Henry went to grab my luggage while I stepped to the front.

Estelle climbed down and gave me a hug, her lip quivering. "Be safe, mademoiselle." The French ladies' maid sniffled against my shoulder.

"We will see each other again," I told her while flashing a smile at Tom. "Who else can style my hair as you do?"

She nodded, her pink lips tight. "Évidement... I shall miss you, mademoiselle. Au revoir."

Henry handed me one of the suitcases. I waved at Estelle and Tom, and then we were off to find passage on a ship.

26

Passage To Cork

"You should pull up your hood," Henry said, scanning the docks. "If the Bow Street Runners managed to send word ahead of us, they might be looking for a dark-haired man accompanied by a blonde woman."

I did as he said and pulled the hood on my coat up over my head. Plumes of acrid coal smoke filled the air above us while tobacco smoke from the many dock workers mingled around us, creating a noxious smell of burning smoke, unwashed bodies, and salt and rotted fish.

"Do you really think they might have managed to send word ahead of our arrival?"

Henry frowned, keeping us close to the wall of an office building near the start of the docks.

"It is better to be safe. We did not spend a lot of time in that bookshop or saying goodbye to your family but still... traveling by carriage during the night will have slowed us down. If the Bow Street Runners sent out a single rider, they could have arrived at the docks with plenty of time to spare."

My gut twisted. I hoped Henry was wrong.

Careful to not draw attention to ourselves, we inched forward along the side of the wall. Henry kept me behind him. So far, I only saw boat crew and dock workers ahead.

"I think the coast is clear." I moved out from behind Henry to turn around the corner when his hand gripped the back of my coat and he pulled me back against him. His chin rested on my shoulder. I turned my cheek so I could see him.

Henry raised a finger against his lips, nudging his head towards a uniformed man with his back towards us. "There is a constable patrolling in that direction. Let us turn in the other direction."

I nodded, keeping my lips sealed. My suitcase weighed heavy in my hand.

"Any sight of them?" Another constable exited the office building, hand resting on a truncheon hanging from his hip, black hat glinting in the dawn-light above his fierce sideburns. My heart thrummed loudly in my chest. How were we supposed to evade them?

"Not yet." The first constable we spotted scratched his chin. My breathing was shallow. "This is the fastest spot to make the journey over to Ireland if the Gentleman Thief decides to skip town, but he could decide to be less conspicuous and travel up to Holyhead or Liverpool or even up to Scotland."

The constable licked his lips and glanced towards his partner. "And what's to say he isn't sticking around, finding a new mark somewhere now that the London season is coming to an end?"

The constable with the mutton-chops thrummed his fingers on the tip of his truncheon, a dangerous looking beating stick. "I hope he'll show up. Be a waste for that bounty to escape us."

I pulled at Henry's sleeve. "Now what?" Those men were too eager for my liking. Henry glanced around. We could not turn left or we would run into the constable nor could we go straight, we would be spotted immediately. I was regretting bringing any luggage with us.

Henry motioned, pointing to our right. Lots of men crossed the docks, constantly busy with their work. If we timed it right, we could hide ourselves within a passing crowd and hide behind the stack of large crates on the other side.

Henry gripped my hand, glancing between the two constables and an oncoming group of dock workers.

"On my count, stay low."

My muscles flexed while my eyes focused on Henry.

"Now."

I ducked my head, joining up with the group of men while Henry did the same.

"Oy!" the constable shouted. I forced myself to not glance back. Henry gripped my hand and pulled me down with him behind the first set of crates.

"Head down," Henry whispered. He held my hand tight in his own while he scooted to the side and peeked around the edge of the crate.

"What is happening?" I asked. My face paled. What if this was it? What if all our efforts had been for nothing and we would get caught this close to finding a boat to Ireland?

Henry kept his voice low. "I see the constable; he-" Henry lurched back.

"What?"

"He looked this way; I do not think that he spotted us."

Careful to stay out of sight, Henry peeked around the corner again. "The constable is following the group of workers. He is stopping them."

"We cannot stay here."

"I agree. We need to continue on." Henry stiffened. "The constable is turning back around."

The constable neared, and I could hear his gravelly voice. "Thought I saw something."

"Think it was him?"

"Let's do a sweep of the docks to make sure."

My eyes widened, and I implored Henry to come up with a solution. We stayed crouched while Henry whispered in my ear. "We can no longer stay here if they come looking. See the warehouse behind us? Follow me."

Henry and I remained low, quietly darting from crate to crate until we reached the entrance to the warehouse. Henry peeked around to check for workers. Besides a few busying themselves adding labels to items in a corner, there was no one in sight.

With a last glance in all directions, we ran straight into the warehouse, not stopping until we reached the back wall. I slid down behind a pallet of what looked like rolled carpets.

"Are we even going in the right direction? Where do you think a boat to Ireland is docked?" I let go of my suitcase and peered over the top of the rolls. I did not see any movement.

"There is a packet boat making regular crossings to deliver mail, but that would be too risky. If there are constables on the lookout, I would wager they have one posted there."

"Then what should we do? Return to London or join a boat to the West Indies?"

"There might be another ship stopping in Ireland. We have to ask someone."

Henry stopped and motioned his hand for me to duck.

"Seen anyone enter?" the constable asked a worker near the front of the warehouse. I could not make out what the response was, but I knew we had to hurry. I gripped my suitcase, and together, Henry and I sneaked past the stored items until we reached a wall on the far side of the warehouse.

"I do not see another door." Henry frowned as he looked to the sides.

I glanced up at the only opening near us; a window about five feet off the ground. I swung the glass to the side and threw my suitcase through the open window then grabbed Henry's and dropped his through as well.

My eyes darted to Henry. "Can you lift me up? We have no other choice."

Henry nodded grimly and weaved his fingers together to provide a step for me.

I planted my feet on top of his hands while he boosted me towards the window. With my upper body sticking out, I managed to turn onto my hip and pull my legs through, dropping to the stone below.

"I am safe, now you. Come on, Henry."

Henry heaved himself up through the window. He leaned

on the sill, lowering his body down on the other side. I grabbed his shoulders to steady him.

"We need to move. If the constables are scouring the warehouse, we might have some time to escape and find a ship." We both picked up our luggage.

Resting his hand at the small of my back, Henry steered me towards the other side of the dock. He stopped a passerby. "Excuse me, are any of these ships leaving for Cork?"

The man finished chewing and spat at the ground. "The Severn's waitin' on slack tide to leave; it'll dock at Cork before moving on to Barbados. I'd hurry, if you want to get on before it sails."

"Where can we find The Severn?"

The man fixed his cap and pointed to the distance. "The large one, third dock down."

"Thank you," I said while gripping my suitcase tight. Henry clasped my hand, and we hurried down the docks.

A large ship loomed before us; its sails were not yet spanned, but the crew had started to position itself by the rigging around the deck. Two men stood sentinel by the wooden walkway, still linking the port side of the ship to the dock.

"Can I purchase passage for two to Cork?" Henry asked. I shifted my legs and set the heavy suitcase down at my feet.

The left shipmate ogled us and scratched his chin. "That'll be up to the ship's master."

"Could you take us to him?"

Following the shipmate up to the deck, I breathed shallowly and covered my nose. The man led us to the stern where a well-dressed older man with ruddy cheeks called orders to his crew.

"Nearly there, men. Ready the ship for disembarking." The ship's master spotted us. "Who have we here, Evans?"

The shipmate pointed his thick thumb at us. "These two are looking for passage to Cork."

The older man inspected us, an intelligent glimmer in his eyes.

"Aye, right on time too. The ship's leaving at slack tide. I suppose we have space for two passengers." He sniffed and held out his hand. "Two quid and you've got yerselves a bargain."

Henry gripped the man's hand and shook while I fished out a bank note from my reticule.

The ship's master accepted the note. "That's settled then. There's an empty cabin below that's yers until Cork, but yer welcome to stay on deck during departure as long as ye keep out of the way of my crew."

I smiled at The Severn's master. "Thank you."

Henry grabbed my suitcase so I could be free to tie my bonnet tighter below my chin, and we took a stand at the railing overlooking the river, wind whipping my hair as I stared out over the docks. The last of the men boarded the ship and the walkway was raised. Behind me, a horn blew while men climbed masts and pulled at the various rigging along the boat, raising the canvas sails.

The sun had risen to a higher position in the sky, taking away the pinks and oranges that had tinged the horizon only a half hour ago. Slowly, the ship steered away from the floating docks, following its path along the river Avon towards the ocean. Seagulls drifted by, crying their choking calls.

I said a bittersweet goodbye to England and turned to Henry. "We made it."

Henry smiled and put an arm around my shoulder. "Let me show you my home."

27

Mo Ghrá

Four days later, Henry and I found ourselves overlooking the grounds of the Duke of Cashel. I rubbed my backside and stretched my cramped legs. Green fields stretched out on either side of the road, bordered by low shrubbery and the occasional tree. Fluffy, white sheep meandered around the grassy hill, chewing the tender green shoots. Before us stood an impressive mansion built long ago so the stones had worn and grayed.

Henry sent the coach driver ahead of us so we could walk the last mile up the hill. These past days we had been confined to a ship's cabin and then, as soon as we arrived in Cork, to the inside of a shared coach. We only had the luxury of a private driver for the last leg of the journey.

My mouth watered at the idea of having a proper meal at an actual dining room table again instead of the bits and pieces we had scrounged up along the way, and a feather bed to sleep on was also an added bonus. Though I was nervous to meet Henry's half-brother for the first time.

Henry clasped my hand and kissed my cheek. "He will love you, like I do."

My stomach quivered, and I briefly wondered if it was too late to turn back before I came to my senses. This was Henry's home and Henry's brother. I was glad to see and experience any part of his life. Hooking my arm with his, we loped along the road.

Turned out I had nothing to worry about; we were welcomed at the entrance to the Cashel mansion by Edmund who looked very similar to Henry. They must have inherited their dark, curly hair from their father.

"Henry, welcome back." The real Edmund slapped his hand on Henry's shoulder blade, a wide grin brightening his face. His gaze turned to me. "And who is this?"

"Brother, let me introduce you to my fiancée, Beth Easton." I smiled a bit abashed.

Edmund's eyes widened and he glanced at Henry with a bemused look. "Fiancée? Does she..."

"Yes, and yes."

"Well," Edmund blinked and shook his head, then he grinned at me. "Welcome to the family; it is nice to meet you, Beth. You must tell me all about how you and Henry met." He leaned towards me and winked conspiratorially. "I must admit, I never thought I would see the day that Henry would bring someone home with him."

"Whispering with my fiancée already, Brother?" Henry lifted his brow.

"Of course, if she is to be my sister-in-law." He waved at

the front door. "Come, let us head inside. Beth might like a tour of the house." Edmund paused and seemed to think. "Or perhaps you might like a moment to freshen up and rest? Henry could show you a guest room and we could meet again at dinner time?"

I was tired and my muscles ached from the journey. I nodded. "I would like that."

"Good, I will have your luggage sent up to your room. And Henry," Edmund glanced at his brother with a certain expression that said he knew what Henry might be thinking. "I will see you in the sitting room as soon as you've seen Beth to her room?"

Henry shrugged and smiled serenely. "Of course, what else would I do?" What else indeed. After constant travel, I would not mind spending time alone with Henry in a comfortable room. My cheeks flushed at the thought, and Henry could not hide the smirk on his face when he detected their reddened color.

"I will be right back," Henry told his brother. He showed me to a spacious room on the second floor. Thick padded rugs with burgundy and gold patterns lined the wooden floor. A slight chill permeated the room, but the luxurious sheets covering the double bed beckoned me. Perhaps I could close my eyes for an hour before freshening myself up and changing into a different dress.

Henry kissed my temple. "Take your time, mo ghrá."

I gazed up at him. "I have heard you say that phrase before. What does it mean?" I tested the sound, trying my best to pronounce what I had heard. "Moe graw."

Henry's eyes twinkled. "Good try. Mo ghrá means my love."

"Oh." His words had left me speechless. My heart raced.

Henry caressed my cheek. "Rest, Beth. I will be back to fetch you for dinner."

I grinned at Henry. "Alright, moe graw."

* * *

Edmund choked back laughter and took a sip of water. "If I understand correctly...you both thought you were other people?" He snorted and cut a slice from a piece of meat at the center of the table.

I bobbed my head. "Apparently we both had been on the verge of confessing the truth, but then Arabella, an acquaintance of mine," I clarified, "outed me."

Henry raised his shoulders and looked apologetic. "And I thought I was doing the right thing by pushing Beth away when she came looking for me. My situation at the time was a bit precarious."

Edmund finished swallowing a bite of food. "I would say so with the Bow Street Runners in high pursuit through the Covent Garden Theater. Perhaps I should go to London more often if it is this exciting."

Henry's brother treated the matter lightly, but I would need a few more days to distance myself from the frightful affair. I turned to Henry. "Say, did you ever manage to get what you wanted from Ms. Chapman?"

Henry winked as he poured me a glass of wine. "Ms. Chapman has misplaced a certain necklace."

"Let me guess, the same necklace is now in your possession?"

"You would have guessed right."

I inclined my head and thoughtfully chewed a slice of spring lamb. "That means that at least some good has come from your time with her."

Henry's dark eyes fixed on me. "Do I detect some jealousy?"

I lifted my chin. "Not at all."

Edmund laughed. "I take it the first bann will need to be read by our vicar this coming Sunday."

My ears burned. Three weeks, that was all it would take before the three banns would be read and Henry and I could marry. "My brother and his wife are planning to make the journey to be here for the wedding."

The dinner passed by without a hitch. I genuinely liked Henry's brother; the prospect of getting to know Edmund and Henry more delighted me. After a night cap in the drawing room, I exchanged good nights and returned to my bedroom. Henry had his own chamber at the other end of the hall.

A maid had lit a few candles in the room; one on my nightstand, one by the washing basin, and another at my vanity, bathing the room in a soft golden glow. The room made me feel like a medieval princess with its exposed beams on the ceiling and the worn-down stone walls. There were even tapestries hanging from the ceiling. I sat down on a short bench in front of the vanity mirror, rolling out my fastened hair, blonde locks falling down between my shoulder blades in soft waves.

I was about to undress when someone knocked on my door.

"Beth," Henry's voice whispered. "May I come in?"

My heart skipped a beat. Henry...at my door, at night, and this time there would be nothing and no one to disturb us. There was no reason to wait until our marriage night to consummate our love. Henry wanted me and I him. I opened the door, skin flushed.

Henry's gaze darkened, and his Adam's apple bobbed as he cleared his throat. His eyes trailed along my body; his voice turned hoarse with desire. "Beth, from the moment I met you, you have been my undoing." He reached for me, touching a loose strand of hair that had fallen to the front. "You drive me mad, and I need to know, before I proceed, do you want this?" He paused, waiting for my response. His stare made me feel vulnerable and raw; regardless, I needed the space between us to disappear. I wanted to feel him against me. I needed Henry to finish what we had started that day in the room near the London docks.

"Yes." My breath quickened and I licked my lips.

Henry's shoulders relaxed, and then before I could so much as squeak, he pulled me in tight, crushing his lips against me, the musky scent of him filling my nostrils. He swiped his tongue inside my mouth, clashing with my own, making my mind go blank as I molded against him. He raked his hands down my soft curves until he cupped my behind, thumbs pressing into my skin. His manhood stiffened and throbbed against my stomach.

Henry nipped at my bottom lip. "I am going to undress you now."

I nodded, fluttering my lashes.

Henry lifted the baby blue, striped, linen dress up over my head and stepped back to admire me. I stood before him in my chemise and stays, my breasts heaving against the stiff fabric. His awed gaze made me feel like the most beautiful woman on earth.

"A ghrá mo chroí, my heart's beloved."

Henry's strong hands returned, caressing and touching the skin on my neck and arms, leaving a tingling sensation wherever I felt the touch of his hand. He slipped his fingers around the hooks on the back of my stays and let the garment fall away, releasing my breasts. The only thing between his touch and the rest of my bare skin was the thin, knee length chemise I was still wearing, though, it did not do much to protect my shape from his gaze. Henry's eyes darted to my breasts, the pink peaks visible and hardening against the cotton chemise. His hungry stare delighted me, and I decided I needed to see more of Henry.

"I want to touch you."

Henry grabbed my palm and placed it against his chest. "You may touch me wherever your heart desires."

I bit my lip and slipped my hand beneath his shirt, teasing my finger along the ridges of his abdomen and up his firm chest. "Here?" Henry closed his eyes and nodded. I nipped at the lobe of his ear. "Here?" He nodded again. My attention turned to the outline of his manhood. I had never touched another man like this before. Slipping my hand lower until I felt the bulge strain against my hand, I murmured, "What about here?" Heat radiated from his body as I cupped him firmly.

Henry groaned, his eyes flashing open. He pinned his arm around me and kissed me hungrily, lifting me up so I had to wrap my legs around his waist. "If you continue that, I will not be able to take my time with you," he growled.

I giggled against his mouth. "Perhaps I do not want you to take your time."

Henry carried me to the bed and deposited me onto the

silky covers, tearing the chemise away from my body, so I lay bare before him. He smirked as he lifted his right arm and pulled his shirt up over his head, ruffling the dark curls, then he discarded his trousers. I drank in the sight of him; the smooth planes of his chest, his strong muscular thighs, and, lowering my eyes, his large manhood. Henry was a work of art. My breath hitched when my eyes met his again.

Slowly, Henry lowered himself on top of me, his kisses searing my skin as he lowered his head until he popped a puckered nipple into his mouth. He swirled his tongue, teasing and tasting, a deliciously warm sensation spreading through my body and settling between my legs.

Henry propped himself up on his elbow, soft candlelight reflected in his eyes. He looked at me as he lowered his hand, skimming along my navel until his fingers reached the short curls at the apex of my thighs. My mouth rounded into a silent O as he slipped down, exploring and teasing along the seam.

I squirmed. The heady sensation of Henry touching my most sensitive parts rushed through me, flushing my skin. I opened myself up to him further.

Henry kissed the side of my jaw. "Beth," he choked out. "You are magnificent." His fingers slid along my moistened flesh, circling the bundle of nerves between my thighs before dipping inside me, filling me. He added another finger, stretching me in a way that sent tingles up my spine. Henry licked the side of my neck, his short stubble brushing my skin, while he pulled his fingers out and dipped them back in.

I moaned, rocking my hips against him. Henry captured my mouth, our breaths mingling. He pushed the heel of his palm against the bundle of nerves, a pressure building in my core.

"Don't stop."

Henry's motions quickened until my breath hitched and my body spasmed against his hand. Jolts of lighting shot through every fiber of my being and I melted underneath his kisses.

2 8

Vows

My stomach fluttered as I waited outside of the chapel at the base of the hill. My hair was curled and fastened at the crown of my head; spring flowers weaved through so that white daisies peeked out from my blonde locks. My cheeks turned a shade of pink, lending color to the white lace embellished dress I was wearing.

I gripped the bouquet in my hand tighter and turned to the open doors.

It was happening. After today, I would be a wife, Henry's wife. My fake Irish duke was waiting for me at the end of the stone walkway.

I chewed my lip as I entered the sunlit chapel, my palms sweaty beneath the cream gloves. On my right, John and Rose beamed at me from their pew together with Anne and Willa. Anne beamed at me and waved. Their support helped settle some of my nerves. Edmund sat in front of them, smiling back as well. The other seats were taken by locals of the parish, excited to witness a wedding, especially when the Duke of Cashel was opening up his home for refreshments after.

My gaze fluttered to Henry, and my heart drummed. Sunlight spilled through the window, glinting off his dark hair and highlighting the expression of worship on his face. His eyes met mine with such hunger, it felt almost sinful with the parish priest nearby. I blushed, striding towards him.

Our hands brushed as I stepped beside Henry, warmth spreading through me at his touch. My heart leaped with anticipation.

"Mo ghra," Henry whispered to me.

The priest turned towards us. "Now that we are all gathered here today; Henry Fielding, will you take this woman as your lawfully wedded wife?"

As soon as the parish priest finished his sentence, Henry blurted out, "I do."

The priest nodded. "You may say your vows."

Henry turned to me and grabbed my hand, his eyes locking eyes with mine. His eager expression had taken on a deep sincerity. He swallowed. "I, Henry Fielding, take you, Beth Easton, to be my wife, to have and to hold from this day forward, for better, for worse, for richer, for poorer, in sickness and in health, to love and to cherish, until we are parted by death. This is my solemn vow."

I had held my breath during his vows, but now I exhaled with a watery smile, moisture forming at the edges of my eyes.

"What say you?" the priest asked me. "Will you take this man as your lawfully wedded husband?"

I smiled brightly, beaming up at Henry. "I do. I, Beth

Easton, take you, Henry Fielding, to my husband, to have and to hold from this day forward, for better, for worse, for richer, for poorer, in sickness and in health, to love and to cherish, until we are parted by death. This is my solemn vow."

"I now declare you husband and wife."

Henry lowered his head and kissed me to the cheers of everyone present.

* * *

"That was a beautiful wedding," Rose said as she clinked our glasses together in celebration, mine filled with a tart white wine while she sipped juice. She patted her lower stomach. "Now a wife and soon to be auntie, I hope you and Henry will visit Hawthorne soon. Little Hyacinth or Laurel will need an aunt and uncle."

I giggled. "Laurel? I thought you had settled on Violet or Lily, or perhaps Oleander if it's a boy."

Rose shrugged and smiled, eyes twinkling. "It is still a work-in-progress."

"Perhaps we can help come up with some... other options?" Anne laughed and sipped her wine.

Rose lifted her brow teasingly. "Hyacinth not to your liking?"

Willa popped up from the refreshments table with a small pastry in her hand. "I like it."

I glanced over to the refreshment table where Henry was having a conversation with John and Edmund. Everyone attending the wedding had followed us to the back garden of the Cashel's mansion and were now mingling and enjoying the spread of food and beverages. Henry's eyes caught mine, and he tipped his head, a smirk on his lips. I already had a taste of what to expect and his darkening gaze told me he was remembering the same thing.

"Looking forward to your wedding night?" Rose lifted her brow when she caught my blush.

"Perhaps."

Rose bumped against me in a teasing way. "Yeah, I'm sure." She laughed. "Did you know that Tom and Estelle are also engaged?"

"No?" The news delighted me. I had been aware that Estelle liked the coachman but engaged? I had not expected that.

"They broke the news when they returned from dropping you and Henry off in Bristol. Tom's resigned from the house in London and now works at Hawthorne. Estelle and Tom moved into one of the guest rooms until their new home is built."

"I cannot wait to see her and congratulate her." I supposed this London season had proved fruitful for my ladies' maid as well as myself.

My gaze flitted to Henry. He cast a handsome figure in his tailored jacket. He sipped some wine from a glass while he laughed with John.

"Let us join our men," I told Rose, leaving Anne and Willa near the refreshments. We linked arms and walked to Henry, John, and Edmund.

Henry swung his arm around me and pulled me against his side. His lips brushed my cheek. "Hello, Mrs. Fielding."

I leaned into his kiss. "Hello, Mr. Fielding."

Having my family here to support my marriage to Henry made me happy. When I set out for my first London season, I would have never imagined to find myself in Ireland, married to the Gentleman Thief no less. But here I was, and it was glorious.

Afterword

For everyone reaching this page and deciding not to skip the afterword, thank you for reading Beth Through Time. Your continued support means the world to me and if you would like to show your love for my novels by leaving a review on any of the review sites, I would greatly appreciate it. Without your readership and your continued support, I would not be able to write these stories.

Beth's novel was a delight to write, I am glad I could give her the love story she deserved as well as some freedom from her overbearing brother, John. I hope you have enjoyed Beth's journey as well.

As always, a lot of the settings in Beth Through Time were once very real places. If you are interested in the history behind some common Regency England settings, I highly recommend looking them up online. Some of the real places I have included were Gunter's Tea Shop, the foundling Hospital, and the Covent Garden Theater.

Gunter's Tea Shop was a confectionery store in Berkley Square that was started in 1757 by an Italian man named Domenico Negri and was quite popular for its ices, a variety of naturally flavored ice creams. Of course, I figured this would be a perfect place for Beth and her friends and family to go to have a treat and for John to run in to an acquaintance. It was a popular place for the London society to be seen.

With this book, I also delved into research about Regency era maritime history. Fun fact, the ship that Beth and Henry escape on was in fact a real ship that would take off from Bristol. Writing books can definitely take your research into strange places like a shipping ledger from the early 1800s.

If you would like more behind the scenes info you can find more on my website, www.harmkebuursma.com, or you can follow me on social media or sign up for my newsletter. As a bonus for signing up to my newsletter you will receive a spicy deleted scene from Rose Through Time and an adult Regency era coloring page.

If you would like to be one of the first people to get your hands on my latest work, you can also sign up to be a Beta reader or ARC reader on my website or social media.

Thank you and stay reading!

Acknowledgments

The publishing of Beth Through Time marks exactly one year into my journey as a published author. The past year has been a whirlwind of new experiences for me. From anxiety about releasing my first novel, Rose Through Time, to becoming a semi-finalist in the Booklife Prize Award by Publisher's Weekly for the same novel.

I have so much to be grateful for when I have done author signing events and have even seen my novel in stores. When I first started publishing, I could never have imagined this much positive feedback and I am incredibly thankful for everyone who has supported me and my books. I promise that there is a lot more coming!

I want to thank my team of beta readers who have read an unpolished version of Beth Through Time and helped me make it the best version it could be. Thank you, Tessa, Jeannie, Brandy, Theresa, Liz, and Anna.

I also want to thank Getcovers.com for another beautiful cover in my A Magical Bookshop Novel Series and Patterson Photography for my author photo.

For editing, Megan Sanders once again worked her magic to polish Beth Through Time until it gleamed. And last but not least I want to thank my husband for doing the unglamorous job of bringing me coffee and treats and reminding me to take care of myself when I need it.

Writing a novel is a lot of work and it cannot be done without the support of those who want to see you succeed.

About the Author

Harmke Buursma is a writer, and author of the book Rose Through Time. She uses her background in Journalism to help bring her fictional characters and worlds to life. When she isn't writing, she likes to read as many books as she can get her hands on. Originally born and raised in The Netherlands, Harmke now lives in Las Vegas with her husband Matthew and two dogs.

Harmke Buursma
Photo by Patterson Photography

For more information about Harmke and her books, visit www.harmkebuursma.com.

Books by this Author

ROSE THROUGH TIME

WILLIAM THROUGH TIME

BETH THROUGH TIME

ANNE THROUGH TIME

Coming Soon

Audiobooks

Rose Through Time now also available as an audiobook narrated by Krista Nicely

Rediscover the magic of the first installment of the A Magical Bookshop Novel series now available on Amazon, Audible, and Itunes.

For more information, check out
www.harmkebuursma.com

9 781737 403395